beyond the glittering world

Praise for *Beyond the Glittering World*

"An enduring collection straddling time, language, and genre. The interconnectedness of the writing and the writers—as Indigenous people, stewards of the land, and keepers of history —serves as the anthology's beating heart."

—*KIRKUS REVIEWS*

"More than a collection of stories, this is a magnificent opus my heart hears in whispers and lee-lees, every chord resonating truths."

—ANGELINE BOULLEY, *Firekeeper's Daughter*

"A map of survival and becoming, drawn by Indigenous hands that remember the stars. These stories burn, bless, and build. They carry our aunties' laughter, our languages, our rebellions, and our love into futures shaped by kin and courage. These aren't just imagined worlds—they're remembered ones. This is the future speaking in its oldest tongue, and we'd do well to listen."

—SHANE HAWK, co-editor, *Never Whistle at Night* series

"A prescription for hope, truth, and a loving heart to all who need a cure for patriarchy."

—CAL CROSBY, The King's English Bookshop

"Reading these stories and poems filled with such strength and beauty, left me feeling echoes of both the ancestors and future generations. These voices braid together to show us how the world is, and how it could be. *Beyond the Glittering World* is medicine."

—HILLARY SMITH, Black Walnut Books

"*Beyond the Glittering World* includes a range of riveting story-tellers whose words reflect and refract. Let this anthology sweep you away!"

—ELISE PASCHEN, *Blood Wolf Moon*

"An evocative compilation of female voices pondering Indigenous futures and the shape of Indigenous love. *Beyond the Glittering World* holds a healthy dose of gender-bending, genre-challenging, future-hoping might. This anthology is a welcome addition to the field of Indigenous anthologies."

—DEBORAH JACKSON TAFFA, *Whiskey Tender*

"These feminisms and futurisms carry a timeless truth: our bodies, our language, movements, dreams, and knowledge are inextricably bound to land."

—SARETTA MORGAN, *Alt-Nature*

"A vital addition to a burgeoning canon of Indigenous feminist creative work. The writers in this anthology write with a beauty and historical consciousness that is inspiring and much-needed in the face of the colonial-capitalist machine called America."

—BILLY-RAY BELCOURT, *Coexistence*

"*Beyond the Glittering World* packs a fierce punch. With a combination of new poetic voices and established favorites, this anthology reminds us that Indigenous feminisms wield language to create intimate and critical spaces to transform the darkness and violence of colonialism and capitalism into nurturing worlds of strength, power, and life."

—DR. MISHUANA GOEMAN,
Professor and Chair of Indigenous Studies, University at Buffalo

beyond the glittering world

an Anthology of Indigenous Feminisms and Futurisms

edited by Stacie Shannon Denetsosie,
Kinsale Drake, and Darcie Little Badger

TORREY HOUSE PRESS

Salt Lake City • Torrey

Published by Torrey House Press
Salt Lake City, Utah
www.torreyhouse.org

International Standard Book Number: 979-8-89092-030-0
E-book ISBN: 979-8-89092-031-7
Library of Congress Control Number: 2024952875

Title from "Beyond the Glittering World" by Shaina A. Nez
Cover art by Lynne Hardy
Cover design by Kathleen Metcalf
Interior design by Will Neville-Rehbehn
Distributed to the trade by Consortium Book Sales and Distribution

Torrey House Press offices in Salt Lake City sit on the homelands of Ute, Goshute,
Shoshone, and Paiute nations. Offices in Torrey are on the homelands of Southern
Paiute, Ute, and Navajo nations.

Table of Contents

Foreword

Natalie Diaz

I'm often not sure *where* or *when* most people are referring to as they invoke *the future*, and yet I understand our need to find a language for our desire to live, an articulation for our yearnings to love and be loved, and continue the relationships with this world and the living beings in it, relationships our ancestors fought for and tended. In Mojave, when we say *tomorrow*, we are also saying *morning*, and both words are a description of the dawn—a silvery smoke-like color that spreads along the chain of mountains around our valley, not quite grey, not quite white, a transformation point at the horizon between night and day, dark and light. Our words for that time and place are *nyamathaam*, *nyamathaav*, and *nyamasaav*. Each exists as an energy beckoning us out of time and clock, compelling us to walk or run toward the great power of the sun. The three words I wrote above begin with the prefix *nya-*, which is a shortened version of our word for sun,‘*anya*. In this sense, *the future* is as imminent to arrive as I am to arrive in it. My responsibility, as a human, is to not sit and wait for it but instead to meet it, through my makings and labors of sleep or dream, or running wild in the night. I'm not saying the future is the sun. I'm wanting to speak of the future as if it moved like the sun, like the sun's light, in that it is here, and we are in it, part of its cycle, not separate from it.

I realize, now that I'm older and live mostly off-rez, how lucky I was to grow up with the knowledge that *future* was something I was already standing in, not a far away or out of reach place, and that it and I would not be deferred. Of course, having just written the word deferred, I am reminded of Langston Hughes' poem "Harlem," which he begins with a question: *What happens to a dream deferred?* In the final lines of the poem, Hughes continues to wonder and then finally demand, which comes with no small danger, to refuse the long wait of that deferral, as he wrote:

> Maybe it just sags
> like a heavy load
>
> *Or does it explode?*

Our word for explode, as well as our words for burst and bloom, is *itpakm.* This is what the sun does when it first rises above our sand dunes: *'anya itpakm.* It is what the sunflower does when it begins to unfurl, all crazy-green, from its bud: *ichipaq.* These same energies and life forces of sun and cycle, blooming and desire, are woven through the works in this anthology.

What a gift that Stacie, Kinsale, and Darcie have called back to and forward toward *the glittering world,* which echoes in many of our Native stories and how we tell of our early homelands and home waters, the journeys our ancestors made before us and *for* us. The glittering world is a world we know and also a world we have never met but have been told about, that lies behind us, beneath us, and in front of us. The Mojave glittering or sparkling world is a time when the world was still wet, after a flood or deluge, or after the original waters we came from had receded. It was from this wet and soft land that we were formed, from its mud, clay, and elements. Across our many different Native stories, the glittering world is, among many worlds, one of land, water, and origin, an origin which is/was connected to all the elements and worlds and beings that existed before us. It is also the world into which we had to learn to walk, to stumble, to run, to plant, to fish, to eat . . . to listen, pray, and story . . . to war and love, to recognize our wounds and heal them, to play and make. In this glittering world we are also taught to dream. We have become those dreams. And we have yet to become those dreams. *Beyond the Glittering World* is a rigorous calling from these three generous editors and twenty-two writers to keep meeting the new world and find the language we need to carry the suns of story and song to those we are alongside in this difficult yet astoundingly beautiful and bounteous world.

A sign that a people's language is alive and vibrant is that they can change in it, through it, evolving and growing their memories and stories in that language. Creating new songs. Creating new dreams. To make story is to bring your life and beloveds to bear on this world. The writers in the pages before us are making the new stories we need to tell of what it means to live in this moment and the many moments that add up to our singular and collective existence. The writers in this anthology reach into and through expected or traditional forms of poetry and prose toward forms shaped by their own elemental and communal experiences of the worlds and homes they come from. These are worlds they have known with their own hands and mouths and eyes, and they are also the worlds they have been told of and dreamed about.

One of many threads that weaves these writers together is they each come from lineages that still remember and honor the glittering world, its newness and possibility, its precarity, and all the things that make it worth fighting for. One of the greatest gifts of these stories is that their characters, speakers, and singers are fully aware of what in this world is out to destroy them and the colonial violences that have marked our lands, bodies, memories, and languages. And yet, the stories are not the sum of those things. We are not the sum of those things. These stories and poems and songs are stairways and pathways to who we are becoming, who we have always been becoming, and we become those people by constantly reminding one another of the immense life and wonder and hard-earned love that make this world worth laboring over, imaginatively and physically, in grief and in joy, in rage and in intentional tenderness. Like the sun makes the day, to make story is to make a kind of light.

Introduction

Stacie Shannon Denetsosie,
Kinsale Drake, and Darcie Little Badger

Steeped in ancestral knowledge, Indigenous futurisms imagine the present and the future through narratives that show the distinctiveness of different peoples amid a common process of returning to ourselves. Why futurisms, plural? Because Indigenous Peoples are not a monolith.

We are many and diverse cultures, histories, and present-day realities. Yes, there are certain shared Indigenous experiences—surviving colonialism, for example—but we fought hard to maintain our distinct cultures. There's incredible beauty in this, our variety.

This anthology takes on a number of meanings for us, as writers, dreamers, and community members. It demonstrates in small part the breadth of our art, which far exceeds the pages in any and every book.

In *Beyond the Glittering World*, we bring together Indigenous writers, especially women, two-spirit people, and people of marginalized genders who are underrepresented in literature, whose stories and poems build on a growing movement of Indigenous voices. The first anthology of Indigenous women's writing can be traced back to *A Gathering of Spirit*, edited by Beth Brant (Degonwadonti), published in 1983. We can also trace the power of including marginalized voices in one collection thanks to the tireless work of Cherríe Moraga and Gloria Anzaldúa in *This Bridge Called My Back* (1981), which was a catalyst for queer and Indigenous feminist coalitions and featured early work by Chrystos (Menominee). We have our own poetry ancestors to thank, Heid E. Erdrich, Laura Tohe, and Joy Harjo, for their comprehensive anthologies of works by Indigenous writers in the twenty-first century. Heid's own voice is included here, in her poem "A Statement on Diversity and Inclusion."

This collection also uplifts emerging Indigenous writers, including AJ Eversole ("Diasulo Walks"), Trisha Moquino ("Our Native Languages Survive Us"), and Maritza Estrada ("Efflux"). You'll come away looking forward to full-length collections and debut novels that have yet to be published.

All three of this book's editors come from matrilocal cultures. Our traditional conceptions of gender and sexuality take on a subversive role as they challenge oppressive patriarchal structures. Women, Two-Spirit people, and people of marginalized genders can be incredible leaders and storytellers; in the vein of futurisms, this has been, is, and will always be true.

Some of these poems and stories may contain references or language that is unfamiliar to the English speaker. We believe that making space for Indigenous syntaxes and understandings of language is an inextricable part of a movement that emphasizes the importance of traditions. Indeed, moving beyond what is comfortable is necessary in Indigenous futurisms.

We offer this anthology as a future of literature where we understand, value, and celebrate Indigenous ways of storytelling and knowing. Each piece, in its own way, answers the question:

What lies beyond the Glittering World?

Efflux

Maritza N. Estrada

If in this life,
  if I were to look back
would I be content
  to the experience.

Cicadas rum-hum
  & I'm not sure
if they'll be good to the trees
  this go-around.

I want to be good, a voice
  so deep once said
  & my hands extended as branches out to sea,
   over &
   into new lands
    of the earth.

To live & name a life,
go inward: lonely-blue
  depth & full force
each syllable, want, relic.

The voyagers of earth
  rotate round & over
hurdles & celebrations
often in solo company.

Palpitations & heat waves.
I pass the scenic view in multitudes
to transmit & write verses for this land.

What's good?   When did your heart still?
Where, oh, where did the sun go?
What time is dinner with beloved?

Whereas, the cicadas tune their evening
song, somewhere under earth.

The Rhythm of Becoming

Dominique Daye Hunter

Ni:ska pulls on small mocs
She pulls on small mocs
She pulls on small mocs
She pulls on small mocs

Ni:ska braids her fresh hair
She braids her fresh hair
She braids her fresh hair
She braids her fresh hair

Ni:ska plays in the Sun
She plays in the Sun
She plays in the Sun
She plays in the Sun

Ni:ska learns the old songs
She learns the old songs
She learns the old songs
She learns the old songs

Wa:gatč threads her sinew
She threads her sinew
She threads her sinew
She threads her sinew

Wa:gatč bears her first blood
She bears her first blood
She bears her first blood
She bears her first blood

Wa:gatč fasts on the Earth
She fasts on the Earth
She fasts on the Earth
She fasts on the Earth

Wa:gatč listens and prays
She listens and prays
She listens and prays
She listens and prays

Mahé:i sews on bright beads
She sews on bright beads
She sews on bright beads
She sews on bright beads

Mahé:i nurtures her womb
She nurtures her womb
She nurtures her womb
She nurtures her womb

Mahé:i cycles with Moon
She cycles with Moon
She cycles with Moon
She cycles with Moon

Mahé:i leads them in lodge
She leads them in lodge
She leads them in lodge
She leads them in lodge

Bendision

Ha'åni Lucia Falo San Nicolas

as i leave home again, an ocean's length
away to college, mama hugs me close
and says, *don't forget your prayers.*

i board the plane, stiff between two haole
tourists, ankles damp with the kiss of
dewy sleeping grass, plumeria lingering still.
i peer through a slit window, seen by hills,
bays, valleys that know me as child. doors
latch, our shared air, breath, torn asunder.
i cry grief into my sweater. seatmates sleep,
stare blankly into screens. *i have done this
so many times, why do i still mourn?*

i remember mama's note, and whisper
plainly my intentions:

guåhan,
i pray that you do not forget me
i pray that you do not resent me for leaving your comfort shores,
your warming heat i pray that you continue to keep me safe
even when i am miles and miles away i pray that you watch over
our families, and that our families remain to watch over you i
pray that you stand strong, because our people are doing brave
things to protect you i pray that you hold on, because our chil-
dren are growing in love and defiance i pray that you embrace
me once i come back to you, because i promise i will return

each time we part, gray clouds swell to
heavy downpour, showering rain into mud.
i used to think that you were weeping, sad
to lose another daughter, but just before i
leave your view at takeoff, you remind me
that water is sacred acknowledgement, too–
our most precious blessing.

Dilasulo Walks

A. J. Eversole

If it hadn't been for the new Chickasaw Modern Art installation, I might never have escaped the Dallas Museum of Art.

The night after installation, I creep from my home on the fourth floor, the Indigenous American Art Hall, down the corridor to the Meso and South American spaces. I move with my signature whispering grace, each step cushioned by the soft embrace of my true form, beaded pucker toe moccasins, which mute my presence.

It took me 177 years to cultivate myself into sentience and achieve a people body. That's a long time, no matter what the jade hairpin on the third floor says.

Cultivating is not done lightly; it is hard work to grasp the emotions visitors project at me and focus that energy inward. Resentment is a popular one to use, but I don't want to be cursed, as most objects who retain those feelings tend to be, so I focused on curiosity. I drew it into me with every glance over my long years sitting behind glass.

My room is a stifling space I share with only three other pieces from what is now called the United States. Two baskets and a bandolier bag that was made in the 2000s. A modern infant, doomed to live its whole life in a tomb of glass, just like me. I understand its pain, being myself in a pristine condition and much, much older. Though my two centuries are nothing compared to the ones I am going to visit.

Living in a museum makes the *what-ifs* inescapable, and the biggest reminder is that I live with other objects who at least fulfilled the thing they were made for. Tarnished earrings worn upon wealthy ears, weathered stone effigies used in ceremonies, fraying silk that had once been proudly wrapped around warm bodies.

My greatest tragedy is that I have never been worn. The idea that I will never fulfill my creator's reason for making me is something I work hard not to think about.

My people form looks like my people did, brown skin with long black hair. I'm wearing clothing that was typical of my time, a beautiful red tear dress. The deep crimson color matches the fire-colored bead designs on my deerskin—black, white, yellow, orange, and red. I've even got a black belt around my waist, a water pattern burned into the leather.

I round the corner and walk straight into a beautiful effigy that cultivated into sentience long before I was even made. His people body is colored like mine, but his clothing shows off his Aztec heritage. The feathers making up the mantle draped over his shoulders are colorful blues and greens, their crevices filled with shadows in the dull nighttime museum lighting.

"Did you see it?" I asked. "It's *beadwork.*"

I've never seen beading like mine before in an exhibit, and the new art installation just smells like home. Once, I heard rumors that a silversmith would arrive, bringing in dazzling cuffs and rings studded with turquoise, but they never proved true. I've seen so many traveling European and Asian exhibits, but nothing indigenous to my land.

"Little Dilasulo." The Aztec effigy speaks with a fond smile on his face. Dilasulo is what most of the people objects call me. It means shoes in my language, Cherokee. "I don't know if it's a good idea for you to meet those objects."

Has he not heard me? Does he not understand what I mean by beading? The colors might match mine. "Why not?"

"There is danger in exposing yourself to the new," he says, fingers fiddling with his tunic. "You might want to join them, you might wish for things that can no longer be."

"You would know," says a pair of ancient gold earrings lounging along a bench set up in front of an ancient jaguar statue. Their body is masculine in a soft way, and they share the same twinkle in their eye that gleams on the gold of their true form when under the spotlight. I think they're old enough to be Olmec. "You've seen many of your people's descendants walk through the halls and admire you. Imagine leaving your continent, being subject to never seeing your descendants again."

"They exist." The effigy sniffs. "They just don't like to visit small museums in Dallas."

The earrings roll their eyes and sit up, tossing a long black braid over their shoulder and crossing their legs before leaning forward to stare at me.

"If I could, I'd change and throw myself in the purse of the first descendant of mine I see," they say, the glint in their eyes turning sharp and hard, as if reflecting fire. "To be worn again would be the greatest gift. My creator would agree."

"My creator made me for the long walk," I tell them, thinking of the gentle way she prayed over me as she sewed me together. "I was supposed to keep someone safe on their journey. Instead… I got lost in a trunk. Then I was claimed by the settlers. One of them tried to wear me, but I was too big for her feet."

"Dilasulo, you are safe here." The effigy rests a hand on my shoulder. "Go visit that lovely jade hairpin you spend all your time with, let her tell you stories a thousand years older than yours and learn that living in a museum is an easy life."

The earrings jolt forward, pushing up shoulder to shoulder with the effigy. They rest a hand on my other shoulder. "I have one regret in my life," they say in a vehement opposition to the effigy. "I met a descendant of my creator once. I could feel it in my bones. I saw them in his smile. I wanted to leave then, but didn't. Soon after, a curator moved me to this continent and now my odds of finding that line are nearly impossible."

The effigy lets out an indignant sputter. "You are admired

here! The visitors adore how colorful and uncreased you remain. You are displayed in luxury, you've practically got the room to yourself." He eyes the earrings pointedly at this, a scowl on his lips.

"We don't belong in museums." The earrings' brilliant eyes meet mine. "We weren't made for it."

"You think I should, what, jump in the artist's bag and go home with her?" I ask them.

"I think you'll regret not trying," they say with a shrug. A corner of their mouth hooks up in a smile. "But it's up to you. You were cultivated with curiosity. Could you live with yourself if you didn't check it out?"

I want to say more, but a ceremonial mask near the entrance to the hall gives a whistle that the security guard is coming, and we all scatter back to our displays. As the guard makes his way through the rooms, the sense in the earrings' words begins to sink in. I begin to form my plan.

The installation is to happen over three nights. On the third night, the artist herself will be there to oversee the hanging of the focal piece. This is when I take my chance. I hover outside the room waiting for an opportunity to greet her alone.

My moment finally comes far past midnight. The summer sun's early rays slowly flood the atrium adjacent to her hall as I creep softly inside.

The artist walks slowly through all the displays of her work. Beaded portraits of Native women hang between belts and medallions. The pieces are a mix of modern and traditional and reflect the beauty of their creator. Her long hair is light brown, her skin pale, but I can tell without seeing her face that she is mine. Alone, surrounded by her art, she glows with the power of the Creator.

I am unprepared for how captivating I find her. Maybe it is because I am a creation too, that I can understand why we adore those who make us.

She runs her hands over a beaded cuff, turning it just slightly to display at a different angle. I wonder if she has ever worn it; her wrists look slender, perfect for adornments.

The thought makes me suddenly shy. What if she considers me too old? Too out of fashion? What if I just remind her of everything our people have lost?

I have just decided to flee when she turns around and catches sight of me. She gasps, dark eyes widening. One of her hands flies to her chest before she lets out a laugh.

"You scared me," she says before stepping closer. I take a deep breath to fortify my courage and move closer as well. When she registers my clothing, her lips part infinitesimally.

"You're beautiful," she breathes, then immediately flushes. "I mean, your clothes. Your tear dress. It's lovely."

"Wado," I say, thanking her in my own language.

"You're Native?" she asks. "Who are your people?"

"The Aniyunwiya. The Tsalagi. Known now as the Cherokee."

The way I speak reveals something to her. Her study of me turns thoughtful. Her gaze moves down to the moccasins.

"Oh my god, did you bead those?"

I shake my head as she bends down to look at them closer. My face heats at the scrutiny of my true form. My instincts tell me to preen.

"Do you like them?" I ask.

"Of course, the stitching on them is so evenly spaced, and I've never seen beads quite like those. A work of art. Where'd you get them?"

My mouth goes dry. She's called me a work of art. Of course I am used to such language, but most say it as if it would be a shame to wear me. To get me muddied or lose a bead. She admires me, but would she touch me?

I ache to be worn. I want to get dirty. I want to lose some beads to a long stroll. I want a life well lived so desperately that it brings tears to my people body's eyes.

The artist notices immediately upon straightening. "Oh! Are you alright? Did I upset you?"

"It's just… art should be admired, but shoes should be worn. Even beautiful ones. It's what they were made for."

This human, the artist with the Creator in her blood, softens toward me. She reaches out to run a hand over my bicep and cup my elbow.

"Of course," she says and pulls me toward her displays. "This cuff? It's already been bought by a Seminole jingle dancer. It'll go right to her after this display. And do you see this medallion over here, the green and blue one? A Shawnee fancy dancer bought it for his son. None of this art is staying here permanently."

Joy fills me. These pieces will live wonderful, cherished lives. How beautiful for them. If she notices that this makes me just as emotional, if not more, she doesn't say anything. Without having to elaborate she understands my fears of our people's art being trapped. The aftermath of our apocalypse.

Quietly, softly, she leads me on a private tour to see each piece, telling me where it is going, what home it will have. Until she stops beside a necklace and earrings. Technically, they are very basic, but the fire color design catches my eye. White feeding to yellow, to orange, to red, and finally to black. My colors.

"And this set is mine," the artist says. "What do you think?"

I think that I match this set and have an answer to the question in my heart. The future opens up to me, bright and exciting, and hopefully gloriously muddy.

Months later, when the artist packs up her installation and leaves the museum for the last time, she proudly wears her own work upon her neck and ears, and matching moccasins on her feet.

How to Crush a Butterfly in Three Steps

a guide by Samah Serour Fadil

STEP ONE

Forget to feed the chrysalis as it forms. Once the transformation is complete, protect the butterfly as it crawls out of its cocoon by holding onto its wings gently so it cannot fly away too quickly. Be careful because you may hurt it if you hold on too tight. Please remember not to hold on too tight. Still, you hold on too tight.

STEP TWO

Take the anger you've been holding in for generations and project it on your newly discovered bug. Watch your baby moth as it disconnects from reality and funnels its anger—your anger, mama's anger, baba's anger, sister's, brother's, grandmother's, others—into a single flip-flop that smashes a monarch perched on the fence. They thought a bug had no right to sit there. No one told them that insects could be beautiful. No one said insects were deserving of love. No one said the crunch of the wings underneath the warm rubber would harden in their minds like wet cement.

STEP THREE

Watch in silence as they crush 50 mg of promethazine to stop the hallucinations and grind 3 grams of Afghan Kush to ease the pain. Pray as you watch them take things you don't recognize. Recognize that you haven't prayed in so long you've forgotten how. Ask for forgiveness instead. Witness the bug rushed to urgent care as words implode—fists explode—they have an episode, a violent overdose. Pray again as your family spends Eid wondering if the little insect is going to make it out alive from that self-induced coma. Even if we knew it rested best in its own cocoon—even if the cocoon is a coffin of our own making.

Mānoa

Ha'åni Lucia Falo San Nicolas

In ʻŌlelo Hawaiʻi, Mānoa
means thick, solid, deep, vast.

There's a wind that whispers
me home, holds my thoughts
and dreams in their mists.

In the womb of the valley,
they sing comfort, promise,
hope to a homesick daughter

of the Pacific as if they know
within their layered soil
and trenched hills that we

are kin, familiar from cordage:
the umbilical of our creation.

Our Native Languages Survive Us

Trisha Moquino

"Huk sah Hah!" I say in our Native language—one should always know what direction they are going, according to Keres. Walking east, toward the sun, hope bursts out of my chest. My morning had me in the garden, the thin ozone layer and greenhouse gasses making us burn and swim in our sweat. I hovered over our plants, who showed off their humidity, exuding hues of green gas. The good hue.

My people have survived settlers (the invaders, really), Catholicism, boarding schools, Coca-Cola, and climate change. I take in the scent of my great grandparents' home, adobe sand swirled with rain. When I was small, I used to want to lick the walls because they smelled so good. Sweat runs down my face as if we had received the blessing of rain. And yet, it hasn't rained in a summer month. But at least it has started raining more regularly again. Our duty as Pueblo people is to talk to the clouds, to respectfully motion them our way, and we have always done our duty. Drinking Coca-Cola has never been part of that duty. We can't drink bottled or canned anything anymore, as there is not water to waste. The thermometer on the wall indicates 110 degrees, still an unusual temperature for our ancestral lands. We ALL have to keep talking in our Indigenous languages to the land, waters, clouds, and sunflowers. My great grandma, Yah, tells me the natural world stopped listening to English in 2094, twenty years ago.

I greet Yah, hugging her. A whiff of her usual smell rises through my nostrils: hot tortillas coming of the stove and some smokes. "What did you do today?" I ask.

She presses her eyebrows up at me. "Shruthuknee, the same, I smoked, made emaree, and I sewed."

I laugh, remembering a core belief of our people. "Women are not supposed to smoke," my mom once told me. But Yah smoked. Yah, eighty years old, her brown skin kissed by the sun, her energy innocent, yet fierce. So fierce, she once led the fight to have our language in schools. Her leadership was one of the ways our matriarchy persisted. The patriarchy that infiltrated when the conquistadors and Catholics first came through, over six hundred years ago, did not totally win.

"Shuwamihtz," Yah said, "the Kashsteruu tried to stop our ceremonial dances and keep us from praying with cornmeal in our languages. They made our people build their churches and then tried to make us pray in them." And yet, we are still here talking Keres, and women are still leaders, leading many efforts and sustaining stuff, time immemorial stuff.

"Yah," I said, "you are a badass, and I am glad your great-great grandma saw the brilliance of the matriarchy and believed in what could be. She held on to her vision of seeing our Native languages thrive again."

Yah always sits by the fireplace, even in the summer. She looks up from the dress she is sewing by hand.

"Ah stah no hoh meh-meh?" I ask.

Yah is great at answering a question with another question. "Aku hey-key ku-trah-meh-meh?"

Meh-meh, my brother, floats through my mind. Meh-meh is twenty-three years old, five years older than me. "Fuck!" I cry out; I forgot I was supposed to meet him in Santa Fe. We are supposed to go up to watch the green corn dance in Ohkay Owingeh, the place of the strong people, a historic meeting ground for all the Pueblo Natives, a people so powerful that they led the Pueblo Revolt of 1680. All of the Pueblo Natives started visiting Ohkay Owingeh in the 2090s, right before I was born. They went there to be reminded of their strength. In the

2090s, the natural world stopped letting the Mericanahs extract coal and gas for cars and electricity, so they had to walk everywhere. Walking to Ohkay Owingeh to pray and remember our strength reminds our people we can all be strong like the Ohkay Owingeh. Thinking about going to the double O today, my heart flutters as fast a hummingbird's wings; I'm happy that the Rail Runner is functioning again.

"Yah, I gotta ride my bike to the Rail Runner right now so I can catch the train!" It's been a year since gas has run out, and we can only use the old electric car. That is, of course, when we have electricity.

Yah snickers, "The Mericanahs could no longer ignore the heat of the sun lasering down on mother earth, just like our people could no longer allow the explosion of the earth for natural resources." Yah lifts both hands, making air quotes as she says, *natural resources.*

"Creator made them listen." She giggles, and then says, "Hinah sah, shrahmee." Shrahmee, as in *be careful, be respectful to all you come in contact with.*

My chest heaves a sigh of relief as I ride out of the village, smiling because goat heads with their stickly, prickly thorns do not flatten my bike tires. Many of the adobe homes have withstood the heating of the earth. HUD homes, not so much. Yah would always say, "The US government went the cheap route and didn't want to use adobes with those homes. They never keep their promises."

Sweat rolls down my back as I ride the five miles over to Wadi, where the Rail Runner still stops after one hundred years of operation. I really don't know why the area is called Wadi—another piece of history I need to learn, as it might save us. Yah says that her great grandma always used to say the old trading post there in Wadi was visited by Steven Spielberg, the movie producer of *E.T.* It woulda been cooler if it had been visited by Sterlin Harjo, the Muskogee Creek producer of the first all-Native cast prime time show, *Rez Dogs.*

I hear thunder from afar and I raise my hands to the sky. The thunderous sound is coming from the mountains to the west. I look up and I see the rain clouds rolling in. I pray to them and ask if they might rain on Ohkay Owingeh for their feast day today, as that is what they will be praying for. We all desperately need the water. The drought has been persistent since before I was born, right as the 2000s came knocking on the 2100s.

I see a bundle of sunflowers; Ohkay Owingeh people call them Than-Povi in their language of Tewa. Than-Povi was my great-great grandma's name from her dad's side; he was from the Ohkay Owingeh and Hopi Native Nations. I stop to talk to Than-Povi, admiring the yellows that mirror the sun. The sunflower is bent towards the sun, and its beauty hurts my soul because even though it doesn't have to share its strength or beauty, it does. It's unselfish like the sun. I ask the sunflower to stay with us, please. Do not go away again. We need its beauty, its dye, its medicine. In that moment, I wonder why the sunflower's buds always bloom at the top. "Hamash nushk-shromah," I say to the sunflower as I hop back on my bike, "I hope to see you again when I get back home." The sunflower's ray florets, flowers in their own right, sway. It feels like they are agreeing with me, and I wish we had phones like my great grandma said they used to have to take pictures.

There are a few other people who hop on the train with me. We all honor each other, seeing each other, by a greeting in Keres. I see a guy who is about my age, sixteen or seventeen, and we wave. We don't look away from one another like colonialism tried to teach us to do. The Rail Runner glides out of Wadi, and it goes under the old interstate highway. The asphalt has started to crack, and people are afraid to drive on it. I look out at the hills as they turn to a plain of grass, and some areas of the land are parched. The parcels of land that are green with life are where many of us went out and talked to grasses and plants and loved on them in our language. The still-parched parcels are areas hard to reach. There is a lot of land to cover, and while there are many more people today who speak our Indigenous languages, we still need more. We need speakers to help breathe life back into our mother so she can thrive like she used to.

Thirty minutes later, the train rolls into the Santa Fe Depot where Meh-meh is supposed to meet me. He works at the All Pueblo Languages Immersion School on the north side of Santa Fe as a Keres Native language immersion teacher, a highly sought-after job these days. Our Indigenous languages were born from the lands we live on, and the way we talk to the lands in our languages enables us to survive the searing sunrays. Meh-meh took after our great grandma, who helped to open the first Pueblo language immersion school back in the early 2000s. Our languages are in demand now because of the Indigenous knowledge they hold. You can't talk to land, clouds, plants, and sunflowers through English anymore. They won't listen.

Meh-meh is standing on the platform with a young woman who must be Pueblo because she is short and has bangs and long hair. I wave from the window, and they come sit by me.

I whisper to him in Keres, "Why didn't you tell me she was gonna hang out with us? Remember, we can only get into Ohkay Owingeh's village if we speak our Native language." They do that to protect their survival, as some of their natural plants start to wilt if they hear English.

Meh-meh, turning toward the woman, grits his teeth, elbows me, says, "Dang it," and smacks his head.

"Tallulah, meet my sister Shuwamitz," he says. "She reminded me that you can enter Ohkay Owingeh only if you speak your Native language. Do you speak Tiwa?"

Tallulah looks nervously at Meh-meh, and she says, "The last speakers of my Tiwa language are gone. We are desperately trying to learn from our sister villages, but it is slow, especially for the adults. The children are learning it easier. But us young adults, we are trying. We know our lives and the land's life depends on it." Her voice quivers and tears well up in her eyes.

I look at Meh-meh.

"She says she is trying," Meh-meh says to me in Keres.

"Yeah, I know, but will that be enough?" I say. I smile at Tullulah. "We have to believe it is. We have all been trying for hundreds of years." I look at Tallulah, and softness washes over my heart. I tell her, "Let's all go. But Tallulah, you have to promise not to speak any English, or you will hurt their plants."

Tallulah's eyes glimmer with hope as tears roll down her face. She nods, looking at Meh-meh, who squeezes my hand and puts his arm around Tallulah. The Rail Runner soars off to the north.

La Posada Inn

Kinsale Drake

Winslow, AZ

Lost in the heat of a Mary Colter dream,
the passengers load up, four to a table in the azure
air-conditioning of the Turquoise Room.

In the evenings, ghosts of Harvey Girls walk their sure
routes from the kitchens to the patrons, topping
off ice for bullet-cold margaritas and toting desserts.

They come for the trains, those dark horses stopped
only when the wheels ran clean off
and the 40, after Route 66, sliced the slickrock

and shut the town out of business—a loss
that only lasted some decades before Glenn Frey
rocked it back on the map. Of course,

we are speaking of tourists. *Béésh Sinil* (if they
bothered to learn her first name) glows iron-
hot in August, and my best friend laughs out *jiní*

with her hair undone. Midday and she's driving, Kiowa,
to be exact, as we spill out the windows
along the same pot-holed highways

movie stars avoided to die rich in bed under rose-
colored eaves, turquoise dripped from their ears.
In the backseat: her brother's guitar, the remains

of sandwiches warm in their makeshift container.
Normally, I would never let her drive, knowing
the stories of the backroads, rangers

with sunburnt faces and hands that fly quick
to their holsters. She peels onto main street slow,
passing cowboy boutiques and red brick

buildings painted to appear older than they are. Swallows
dip and weave above our heads. We crank our tune
higher, believing ourselves true followers

of the desert. Steel guitars and rattles bloom
from our minivan anointed with bugs. Then we park,
walk the lazy half mile to the Turquoise Room,

where the bilagaanas sport endangered coral, remark
on the pottery, the silver, the glorious paint: *Where
are the rest of the beautiful cars?* A bartender

points with his forefinger out into the glare
of the afternoon, where, we guess (our
mosquito lips sucking up prickly pear

lemonades) the last great Harvey train car
rusts in its lonely exhibit. Constellations
once dotted the ceiling of the car, stars

strung together—a sight, surely, for a nation
thrust westward by delusional visions
of cowboys, kisses from grateful wives and women,

and the prospect of land—that legalized division
of dusty parcels sniped right out from under
Diné families of churro-sheep herders. No way

to sweeten that story. But after slurping
down two sweating glasses, and half
a dry chicken, my best friend's laughter

knocks me silly. *They'll never be as Indian
as they want to be.* We pack up our purses,
leave a tip, and tuck our napkins

just so on the table. White ghosts yearn
from their imported doorways and paintings,
but monuments do little to save us. We sing Eagles, turn

left at the crosswalk, hop back in the van. According
to the compass within me, we still have
many more hours until we settle down into sleep.

Nixtamalización

Ayling Dominguez

27

Yes, the grinding.
But above all, the crack
and splitting of an ear

of corn over her withering
knee, skirted by a pink and yellow
mandil she wears day in and day out,

from milpa to corner store and back
again, her gray, thinning
braid holding out, a volcanic will,

stubborn as the metate and metlapil, she
rolls rock against rock to make
soft, like harvest has always taught.

Alchemize against loss,
nixtamal whispers
even as it is crushed.

In the beginning, it's just you and me against the world

Arielle Twist

In the beginning, it's just you and me against the world.

I don't think there is any glamour in being an Indian mother. Or, maybe I can't comprehend the amount of sacrifice it takes to raise Indian babies in this place that was once paradise, or to rephrase, a place no longer safe for us. This part of the story demands to be witnessed; sacrifice deserves to be heard, untouched. In my beginning, it's just you and me, and though this place is no longer paradise, I find utopia in your arms. I was nothing, and you are everything. Did you know that, mother? I don't have the tongue to speak the language, and english cannot describe the love that I have inherited.

But, still I try.

My haunting will be one of longing
to love something as you have loved me,
to love as imperfect and clumsy as a single mother,
giving all she can give for a better
somewhere,
anywhere, as long as it is with you, little love.

This is me trying to be you,
I've become exhausted,
looking for purpose
love like ours is hard to find

But, still I try.

I want to love with purpose, mom.
I want to love like you've loved me.

It has not been glamorous, I know,
but this story exists because of you.

I want to be innocent again,
or, as innocent as an Indian baby can be

what I mean is that I wish to not know what I know of the world,
but maybe that is naive, the world is still the world,
whether I know or not, right?

I can't tell if I am making any sense?
Like, If the only good Indian is a dead Indian,
then no Indian is innocent, not even the babies

the babies and mothers are the worst Indians,
because they represent life and living.

So, I want to be innocent, but as innocent as an Indian baby,
which is to say I want to invoke living and life
in spite of being the worst, most destructive
disruption in the eyes of genocide

I want to forget the terror that I am, even in my innocence
and nap in my mother's bed on days where I am sick,
which lately, is every day

I want to be small and scared of the things kids fear
like losing my family, or being taken away,
you know? The normal things all kids are scared of

'cause it happens, and I don't want to lose my mom or dad
and even as a little body, my mind reminds me
I could lose them all the time

                              what happens if they don't come home
                    I stand by the window until the headlights pull in

I don't know when I started to stand and wait
or who first told me that moms can go missing or die
I thought moms were forever

                                                    So I wait
                                                and I wait.

and I didn't know where missing moms go
I guess I've always scared of normal kid things
but I don't know how I got to this point

                              I just wanted to be innocent again
                    but now I can't remember a time without fear
          even the invocation of life is scared of it being taken away

I don't know if there was a time I didn't see the world
and how scary it could be as an Indian baby,
maybe I was never that naïve

and still I wait,
for a call or a text
to remind me that I am living

and the world is still the world
whether I know it or not.

Light the Day

Maritza N. Estrada

A land of red mountain
& lost lovers—prickly sand & fallen thorns,

one thousand alacranes marching in translucent bodies,
black curled tails pointing to Huitzilopochtli

reaching for something brighter & brilliant.

We were so lucky
to call this home

home.

Sun Ra's "When There Is No Sun" echoes,
where the speaker is seen exiting one poem

into a continuous desert, lost & bandaging
tender wounds.

Above mountain peak, the boombox
increases in volume, piano & saxophone

crescendos to the sun, to return,
to not let the dark swelling remain.

For something, the speaker returns
to her grave. She buried a box of postcards, letters, fotos,

& one wrinkled red bandana. The passport photo of the lover,
vanished.

We were so lucky to touch & be touched.
In the box, a Mexican rana appeared verde

& pensive sitting on one last note:
In this act of memory & memento,

for who I loved & worried,
here is a part of me

buried & yours.

Sandstone ballad.

Danielle Shandiin Emerson

The statue looked uncannily like her mother. Its nose curved up, stout at the base and plump near the nostrils. Long, straight hair fell below its waist. If she squinted, a part of her was so sure that the statue would start singing—singing in the same husky, saccharine voice Roadside's mother loved showing off at downtown bars.

"What the fuck." Roadside sidestepped and set her flowers down on nearby rocks. She had brought sunflowers—her mother's favorite—though the bouquet felt less important now than it did an hour ago when she spent nearly all morning waiting in line at the Shiprock City Market.

None of Roadside's siblings liked to visit their mother's grave; so, as the oldest, she took the responsibility on herself, reining it in like a wild horse. She'd wake at the break of dawn to greet their mother, hair tied back as the sun warmed her neck from behind. But the grave wasn't much of a grave. There was no headstone, no plot of land. These sandstone fixtures were where they had spread their mother's ashes back when Roadside and her siblings had no money to buy a plot of land in their small-town cemetery. Roadside knew their mother wouldn't care— perhaps she even preferred it this way. She recalled her mother's honeyed voice: *Down between the two-sister mesas where I was born singing, let the wind carry me.*

So, Roadside and her two younger siblings threw their mother's ashes into the sky. The silence made their young ages of seventeen, fourteen, and ten collapse into an aged knowing, where adulthood pulled like wind at their faces. Maybe death wasn't aging. Aging was change. Turning a seventeen-year-old child into a seventeen-year-old guardian. Roadside felt the weight of change against the fine hairs of her cheeks, contrasted by the high sun.

It was a bright day devoid of clouds and shadows. Roadside could barely keep her eyes open. With a gentle heave, Roadside and her brother Dylan managed to empty the cheap aluminum urn, kicking up dirt with their shoes as they skidded back from the cliff edge. They watched their mother's ashes fall in a heavy sheet, trickling like rainfall onto the red sandstone below.

That day, Turquoise, the youngest sibling, swore she'd heard their mother humming. A low echo that seemed to turn the birds quiet. Roadside only heard the soft roar of desert wind turning over dry weeds and dirt. All three siblings stood side by side, hand in hand. Their breath mixed with the sound of cicadas singing in the air nearby. The caws of lingering crows drew their attention upwards toward the sky. They all wondered if those crows carried their mother's soul, soaring above the ashes and into the sun.

When they returned home, Turquoise picked up their mother's old guitar and practiced strumming chords. Roadside and Dylan watched from the kitchen table where they prepared steamed corn stew for the night. With bare hands, Roadside turned over hot náneeskadí before throwing it into a ceramic bowl. Dylan shaped the dough, forming rough circles with his palms just like their mother taught him. For years, all three siblings complained about the lack of space in the house—how things felt cramped and two sizes too small for their growing limbs. That night, everything felt too big. Their mother's empty dining room chair, empty blankets, and empty living room couch made the house feel like it was swallowing everyone and everything whole.

Early on, Roadside came to terms with the fact that she'd never see their mother again. And there was a strange kind of coffee-lined sweetness to knowing that a part of Roadside had found acceptance so quickly. Yet, here she was, face-to-face with her dead mother.

Roadside's eyes ran over red rock looking for another person, or perhaps another statue—anything to explain why there was a near-perfect sandstone replica of her mother. A part of Roadside wondered, *Did someone make this and leave it behind for me?* Roadside took a couple steps closer to the statue.

"What are you?"

Roadside kicked the statue's feet softly, almost as if she expected it to cave with a single touch, to burst into smoke, or fall to the ground like wet rags. Instead, her foot was met with hard, solid rock.

"Jesus." Roadside kicked it again for good measure. It didn't do anything. She circled it, staying at arm's length.

"Mom?" She picked up a nearby stick and threw it at the statue. It fell to the earth. A heavy gust of wind blew it behind the rocks.

The statue remained still. Roadside couldn't take her eyes off of it. Slowly, as if afraid the statue's hands might reach out and grab her, Roadside took out her phone and snapped a picture. The statue looked ethereal in the blinding flash, surrounded by maroon and baby blue. In the photo, she thought the statue was smiling. Roadside instinctively took a few steps back, nearly tripping over her own feet. She looked at the photo, then back up at the statue. It wasn't smiling. Her mother's face was emotionless.

Back when their mother was alive, her family used to call out to each other in a sing-songy voice, laughing at ridiculous variations of each other's names. Roadside used to call her sister Turquoise Turkey. Their younger brother Dylan became Dill Pickle. New nicknames were common, so much so that visitors to their household used to scrunch their noses in confusion. You said her name is Roadrunner? It was an inside joke that only Roadside, Turquoise, Dylan, and their mother understood. Roadside wondered if the statue would respond to her mother's name.

"Lucie?" Roadside said.

Her voice was met with rustling juniper branches and nearby crows. In the sunlight, Roadside thought she saw a shadow move.

"Lucie—"

Roadside was interrupted by humming. It spun in the air, grazing like bluebird talons at Roadside's earlobes and tangling in the thickets of thorns from nearby sage. The humming grew louder and louder until Roadside's legs started to move on their own and her surrounding became a blur.

She ran back to her car, up over a large cluster of rocks and across the wash, kicking up dirt that wafted into her mouth and eyes. In her frenzy, Roadside scraped her arm against passing trees. She winced as thin lines of blood rose from her skin, spreading like red veins. The cuts stung, but Roadside kept running. The further away she got, the lower and lower the humming became until it disappeared completely.

As she jumped in her car, forgetting to slip on her seatbelt, and sped down the old town dirt backroads, Roadside's head vibrated with burning silence.

When Roadside was a baby, her mother sang the most beautiful songs. Her words went high and low, crisper than the winter air that pinched at their cheeks with calloused hands. Roadside's mother used to joke, I'll be singing at my own funeral. In her mind, Roadside expected something showy—perhaps the old local band that her mother used to sing with or even a makeshift stage set up with sparkly boxes and chairs. But on her deathbed, Roadside's mother sang softly, surrounded by beeping machines and white wallpaper.

When I was a girl, I jumped through mother's fields.

When I was a girl, I sang the old songs.

When I was a girl, I refused to keep my lips sealed.
And I twirled and spun and danced all night long.
Now that I'm old, don't let go of my hand.
Now that I'm old, listen to my songs.
Now that I'm old, I know you gotta watch where you land.
As the sun in the sky keeps shining, long and strong.

The morning Roadside's mother died, the hospital was quiet. The nurses and doctors didn't say anything. Their faces were contorted by pity's harsh touch. Even the hallways, which always seemed to bustle with patients and loud click-clackety footsteps, fell to a hush. The world seemed determined to move on, invisible hands clutching Roadside's throat, picking at her skin with sharp nails. She wondered if her siblings felt the same, silenced by their mother's death.

On the hospital bed, their mother was bundled up in multiple blankets. Her hair, cut short and greasy, fell like damp leaves on her cheeks. It was hard to maintain long hair in the hospital, so their mother made the heartbreaking choice to cut it. She forced a smile as she pulled shears from her patched sewing bag. Later that night, Roadside, Dylan, and Turquoise burned their mother's hair in the stove fire; it smelt like sulfur and cedar.

In the pale hospital lights, their mother's face looked flat, and Roadside resisted the urge to shake her shoulders, to scream her name. Roadside held her mother's limp hand tighter and continued the song with her till the end.

When I was a girl, I cried over lovers
When I was a girl, I never ever moved on.
When I was a girl, I hid under covers.
And I wondered how birds spread their wings so far long.

Now that I'm old, I won't forget your kind words.
Now that I'm old, I'll carry the burden.
Now that I'm old, I won't be lost in the herd.
And I'll remember that living isn't always filled with hurting.

When Roadside finished singing, she slowly let go of her mother's hand and folded her arms across her body. Her mother's hair gleamed in the hospital's fluorescent overhead lights. She brushed a bit behind her mother's ear, caressing her right earlobe before pulling away. Roadside was used to seeing their mother's face sunburnt. Their mother spent so much time outside playing her guitar at various street corners that she'd come home dark and sweaty. But here, after weeks in the hospital, her skin was the lightest Roadside had ever seen—a sickly olive that made her hair look jet black.

The doctors hadn't been able to identify what was wrong with their mother, but it was obvious that her health had declined rapidly. When she was hospitalized, Roadside hated to admit it, but deep in her gut she knew that their mother wasn't going to come back out. *It's almost like she made a deal with the devil*, one nurse said, *and that's why we can't help her.*

Roadside remembered an old story their mother used to tell through song, the details fluttering like stars on a blanket not yet molded into constellations. The ending of that story stuck with her. *No one makes deals with the devil for themselves*, their mother whispered. *They do it for the ones they love.*

Before Roadside walked out of the hospital room and into the waiting room where her younger siblings huddled together, she erased this bedridden image of her mother from her memory, choosing to remember their mother as she was singing. Turquoise screamed and cried. Roadside refused to let them pass her. Dylan watched with still eyes from his seat, refusing to stand no matter how much Roadside tugged on his arm. After spending years listening to their mother sing, laugh, yell, scream, all they could hear now was the bedside monitor, occasionally interrupted by a buzz or two from the florescent lights above.

Bzzzt. Beep. Beep. Bzzzt.

A dim echo of footsteps broke the spell, and Roadside listened as their mother slipped on her leather-worn shoes and traveled to the next world. Click. Clack. Bzzzt. Beep. Click. Clack. Beep. Bzzzt. Click. Clack.

Roadside knew that their mother wanted to be a bird. She thought back to stories of Lucie who, as a young girl, whistled tunes back to birds and took time to learn their early morning babbling. From the window, Lucie watched as birds huddled in trees envious of their flock. When left to her own imaginings, Roadside dreamed of feathers springing up like hairs along her mother's arms and legs, black like her ponytail, haloed in the sunlight, and barely touching her shoulders. In this dreamscape, their mother would raise her hands and fall to the earth before flapping once and sweeping up toward the clouds. Roadside thought Lucie would make a beautiful raven.

In the pantry, their mother kept pieces of stationary covered in bird prints and shadows. In weirder places, like behind the toilet seat, their mother kept rotten bird beaks and bones. Roadside discovered the beaks and bones one day after school. She tried to flush the toilet and the water rose. It overflowed and collected at the base of her shoes. Roadside didn't want to call her mom, so she rushed to pull dirty towels and clothing from the laundry basket, hoping the dingy cloth would soak up the water. Once the toilet stopped overflowing and the water mopped up, Roadside returned the wet T-shirts and pants to the basket. The disgusting smell of fresh pee and poop lingered in the air. It took days before the smell disappeared into the washer.

The image of raw bird bones and beaks never left Roadside's mind. Not even while her mother sang songs that invited snow and white feathers—things that were beautiful and pure, not grim and disgusting. Sometimes, Roadside wondered if their mother was a witch. Not the hunched, green witches with gangly brooms, but the scary kind with dry blood underneath their nails and skin-breaking curses on their tongues. The kind of witches that stole locks of hair and didn't hesitate to burn flesh to get what they wanted. The kind of witches that their people only dared to whisper about in sheltered homes, where ceremonies that chased witches away took place. Witches who traded their souls for beauty and talent making deals with beings that walked on four legs.

Roadside never told her siblings what she thought. And she especially didn't ask their mother. She let these thoughts sit like heavy sandstone in her stomach, content to stay like that until something sliced her belly open and the rocks fell out.

Roadside sat with the statue at night, waiting. In the moonlight, the red sandstone took on a white hue similar to freshly fallen snow. A light dusting of moon powder reflecting back shadows that seemed to sneak across rocks in the wind. The statue seemed to fall dormant at night, becoming pure stone—a heavy presence against Roadside's chest. She wondered if the statue depended on the sun for life.

With knees pulled up to her chest, Roadside watched carefully as nothing proceeded to happen. The desert, covered in a dark shawl of silence, matched her breathing. It was strange seeing her mother—albeit as a statue—so quiet, so unlike the dust devil of a woman that Roadside and her siblings knew. She wondered if time would steal away the statue's life and beauty, too—eroded by the same wind Roadside's mother used to dance on and sing with.

After the experience with the statue humming, Roadside thought about the way her mother used to murmur in her sleep like she was humming along to music. Songs Roadside and her siblings didn't always recognize. One morning, Turquoise asked their mother what she was trying to say while sleeping.

Their mother raised her eyebrows. "What?"

"When you were sleeping." Turquoise nodded toward the couch. "Just now."

From the dining room table, Dylan spoke up. "You were humming." His tone almost sounded accusatory, but his face only showcased confusion.

Smiling, their mother threw up her hands. "No idea, darlings," she said and did her best to wipe the sleep from her eyes, before turning to Roadside sitting opposite of Dylan.

"Guess I was practicing for tonight." Their mother winked, and Roadside looked up from her phone. Before any of the siblings could ask more questions or try to recreate the humming, their mother had already swept up her shawl and stepped toward the front door.

"It's gonna be a long show." She slipped on her boots. "So don't wait up for me." And as suddenly as she woke, their mother was gone.

Turquoise stood up and opened the fridge. "Mom made stew earlier." She looked at Dylan and Roadside. "Want me to warm some up for you?"

This memory hurt Roadside's head. They never learned where those sleeping songs came from. And their place in Roadside's memories grew fuzzy each day. It was a wonder that there were still songs Roadside and her siblings hadn't heard before. Or maybe, and perhaps even more curiouser, it was a wonder that their mother made songs up in her dreams. Even while she slept, she created.

Roadside was pulled from her thoughts by an unusual heat from beneath her thighs. The rocks felt too warm, lacking the cool desert blanket that unfurled during this hour. *Maybe,* Roadside thought while she stood, *the warmth wasn't from the rocks, but far, far, far below them.*

The statue remained silent. No humming. For a moment, it looked like her mother's eyes blinked. Roadside wondered if she was in there, trapped in a chamber of stone and shale. For a split second Roadside felt an urge to free her—to break the statue and grind it back into the earth. The heat, seeping through her sneakers made Roadside step back. Their mother loved them; Roadside had no doubt about that, but there were times Roadside questioned their mother's talents. The promises she made and ultimately broke the day she died, haunted Roadside and her siblings. This reunion almost felt cruel.

"Why?" Roadside whispered. "Tell me." She wasn't sure if talking to the statue did anything, though it made her feel vaguely better.

The rocks below her, once warm, now suddenly felt cold. She stood up and tentatively reached out her right hand, cupping her mother's sandstone cheek. Her palm met heat. Surprised, Roadside immediately pulled back. "Fuck."

The stinging brought tears to her eyes, and Roadside felt anger gather like thunderstorms in her chest. "I hope it was worth it," she said and raised her chin, attempting to make eye contact with blank eyes. "You loved us. But you didn't trust us."

Roadside loved her mother but knew she didn't tell them everything. How they got by on a singer's nonexistent salary, how their bellies never experienced true hunger, how scrapes and cuts seemed to heal unnaturally fast. Without knowing it, Roadside and her siblings were locked in a promise, a deal, their mother made with a stranger.

Roadside cracked a sad smile. "And we'll never know if it was worth it because everything died with you."

Waking with the sunrise, watching as light crested over red mesas, the more Roadside thought about the previous night, the more it felt like an old dream.

Before their mother got sick, Roadside remembered sitting in the living room with her younger siblings, listening to their mother play the guitar. *This has been passed down from your grandmother and her grandmother.* Their mother's long fingers strummed the guitar, filling all the cracks in the wall. They had the song memorized. When their mother sang, they sang with her, following the melody like baby ducklings being led to a pond.

From the wings of birds, flying in the sky
To the feathers and beaks, of those singing so high.
I stand with my hands well above my head.
Praying to Father Sky and Mother Earth, that my children
be fed.
That they be taken care of and cherished.
Even when I'm long, long dead.

When I'm caught in the sky, above clouds and the mountains
I want you to look up, and choose love over youth fountains.
To grow old, hand in hand, before we met again.
To fall to your knees because you're just human.
In my absence, please learn to stand straight and tall.
For once you can visit me, we'll shower the earth with
beautiful rainfall.

At their young ages, Roadside and her siblings didn't think much of the song. They simply repeated and harmonized. Even if their voices couldn't hit all the notes, their mother smiled, urging them with a gentle nod to keep going. *Don't give up shi-yazhí, you sound beautiful.* And, while Roadside couldn't shake the odd feeling in her throat—a strange suspicion unfurling like a clenched fist whenever their mother sang eyes closed, almost as if she were praying—Roadside knew that her mother's words were genuine. Even if their singing didn't sound beautiful, they kept going together and that in itself was beautiful. Maybe that's all their mother wanted for Roadside and her siblings: to keep going, and going, and going until they're reunited in the old beauty.

Roadside pondered this as she sang the song softly to herself, stepping over tumbleweeds and broken glass. She scaled dry sandstone and nervously peeked over hills to check if the statue was still there. It was. Nothing about it looked different. It was still a perfect replica of her mother, standing straight and tall. Her mother's hands fell at her waist and her eyes were sharp—the red sandstone somehow recreating the exact light shade of brown.

The statue even adorned her mother's long velvet green skirt, brushing against her ankles, frozen in time. She had on a loose T-shirt tucked in at her waist and wore a light blue jean jacket with bird patches on her shoulders. Their mother loved that jacket. It was a gift from the community, granted at one of their mother's downtown shows. She was buried in that jacket. Roadside had thought she'd never see it again. Of course, the colors were gone, washed out with sandstone, but if she turned her head a little bit to the left, the glint from the sun almost made it look like the beaded patches were still shining like they used to.

When Roadside showed her younger siblings the picture, they all thought it was photoshopped. They got mad at Roadside for playing such an awful prank. It took hours but eventually Roadside convinced Turquoise to visit the statue. She waited in the car. Roadside turned around, a little wary about turning her back to the statue, and waved to her sister, signaling that she could come out.

All those years ago when their mother passed away, Turquoise wasn't old enough to recognize death. On the day of the funeral, she asked why their mother wasn't waking up. Everyone told her to be quiet, to shut her mouth. Roadside tugged her outside, lowered herself to her knees, and taught Turquoise about death. *Mom isn't sleeping. She's not coming back. When you die, you don't come back.* Turquoise still didn't cry. She just nodded her small head and sat in the hallway with Roadside for the rest of the service.

It was a little harder for Turquoise to navigate the rocky terrain, nearly tripping over knee-high weeds and creosote bushes. When she reached the sandstone hills, Roadside extended her arm and helped pull Turquoise up. Her little legs struggled to grip the rock, but soon, she was standing right next to Roadside, albeit out of breath. In a quiet exchange, Roadside smiled and went to let go of her sister's hand. A loud inhale broke the silence and Turquoise's fingers suddenly locked Roadside's hand in a tight grip.

"You weren't lying," Turquoise said.

"'Course I wasn't," said Roadside.

"..."

"What is it?"

"No idea."

"..."

"Can I touch it?" Turquoise took a step closer but was instantly pulled back by her older sister.

"No, we don't know what it is."

"..."

"It's mom," Turquoise said. Something in Turquoise's final and definite voice made Roadside nervous.

"It's not mom."

"..."

Turquoise couldn't stop looking at it. Her eyes were big and glowing. If Roadside weren't mistaken, she'd say Turquoise looked excited. "You said the dead never come back."

"Mom didn't come back."

"..."

"Mom?" Turquoise slipped from Roadside's grip and ran toward the statue. "Mom!"

Before Roadside could snatch her sister's arm, she tripped on a piece of red rock and fell to the ground. A piercing sting erupted from her knees; she'd scraped them. The blood bled through her jeans, turning a dark, dark brown.

"Turquoise!"

Roadside watched helplessly as her younger sister threw herself into the statue, wrapping her arms around its hard surface in a tight hug.

As if cued by touch, the statue started to hum. Turquoise jumped back.

"Get away from that thing!" Roadside grunted as she stood, attempting to pull Turquoise away.

"No! It's Mom!" She struggled against Roadside's grip. "We just need to listen to her. She wants to sing for us!"

"It's just a statue!" Roadside kept pulling, nearly tearing her sister's shirt.

"She wants to sing!" Turquoise pleaded.

Roadside's arms started to ache against Turquoise's weight. Her voice cracked. "There's nothing here!"

The humming got louder and louder until Roadside couldn't hear Turquoise anymore. Panic rose in her throat. *This was a mistake. They needed to get out.* Before Roadside could hike Turquoise up over her shoulder and run for the car, she heard a guitar. It started out softly, so much so that Roadside thought she was imagining it. The guitar strums got louder and more confident. They both froze. The statue kept humming as the guitar churned out an easy acoustic melody. Both girls found themselves stepping closer, waiting to hear their mother's voice. Slowly, as the strumming had begun, it got quieter. The humming grew softer and softer until both sounds disappeared.

Roadside and Turquoise didn't move. They were afraid but also amazed and deathly curious. Around them, the sounds of the desert picked up again: wind picking at dry juniper branches and dirt running across rough sandstone surfaces. Roadside looked at her younger sister, not sure what she was expecting and sure as hell not sure what to say. Turquoise was crying. Tears fell down her face and got caught in her mouth—pieces of snot collected at the base of her nose. Roadside hugged her tightly, lightly brushing her hand through her hair. Turquoise cried for a long time and Roadside held her longer. As they sat like that, tangled in each other's limbs, confused and unsure about everything, their mother's statue watched them. Roadside knew that Turquoise had been holding in her emotions for years, and she wondered if the heat of her tears, heavy and feverish, had set off their mother's statue.

Years from now, Roadside and Turquoise will wonder if they remembered things correctly. Emotions flared like wildfires and confusion ate away at their memories, picking them like meaty bones turned dry. Roadside could only think about the feeling of holding Turquoise as she cried and cried and cried. The walk back to the car was quiet and the drive was silent except for the old static from the radio. Dylan had dinner ready by the time they got back, but neither Roadside nor Turquoise sat down to eat. Instead, they hugged a confused Dylan and moved to the couch where their mother used to sleep during the day.

No one returned to the statue for years. Dylan refused to visit their mother's statue. *It's not good to be near ashes.* Roadside wanted to argue that they weren't just ashes. *It's their mother's ashes.* Dylan stood his ground as stubbornly as their mother's sandstone statue. The scrapes on Roadside's knees healed over into light scars. And Turquoise's tears dried permanent stains along her cheeks. Both girls kept what happened a secret, choosing instead to remember their mother through her guitar. Turquoise spent more time crying than she did smiling, but Roadside knew holding in nearly ten years' worth of tears must have taken a toll on her eyes and heart. While their mother's statue remained a mystery, they never forgot her songs.

Now that I'm old, I won't forget your kind words.
Now that I'm old, I'll carry the burden.
Now that I'm old, I won't be lost in the herd.
And I'll remember that living isn't always filled with hurting.
Because when I make deals with the devil
I make them for you.
No one sells their soul for themselves.
For my love is my only truth.

Roadside did her best to strum the melody on the guitar. From the kitchen, Turquoise and Dylan instantly recognized the song and, lowly, started singing. And somehow, Roadside didn't know how, but deep down, she knew their mother's statue was singing too. Alone but loud, between two sister mesas, ashes fell like rainfall.

Statement on Diversity and Inclusion

Heid E. Erdrich

If I even think about it   a big rubber nothing
    a resistance
          Then somewhere else:
a claim   a stake   and territory overcome   grifted
a loss that's not returned

I'd like to be at that table   where I've been asked so many times
           to take a seat
I'd like to be there that one time   some spirit enters the room
       at last
       and we find relatives in a story
and I am not alone there in the brainpan of institution

We do not trust that healing or wholeness comes from our claim-
ing
        —a presence enters and she claims
claims a brother through a mother   a prior claim   all the way
back

Our seat is brief and only in that one room

One firefly invited to that room   only tells you about the room

                    They   keep saying   healing and wholeness
         I am whole now as I have been ever—
                    broken mixed cracked ruptured
         I remain whole   Whole
            I remain bored with old words   In my head I'm
wholly swept away

There's a place not far from here where fireflies flow downhill at dusk
if you stand opposite that spot   they look like water   They're
not
it's just that the bugs like the warmer air off the bank and lift
from their sleeping places
to move in a group to the warmth above the rocks

Watch the bright flow all you want   It is not what it looks like at
all
They won't tell you anything at all

SWEETHEART

Kinsale Drake

after Lucille Clifton

Miss the pale iris
        when the sky
        blinks

        What
keeps you alive? won't
                you celebrate
                        with me
that pain doesn't
        have to be worthy
        to be felt
& your body
mourns
what it must

All alternate versions
        of your life
        are dead, dead star
        which is
        the first ingredient
        of every beautiful thing
        you can name:

The dew-backed frogs
      or clear cat whiskers
          or snow kissing
    the blue shell
of sky

That there could be
a self
so freely
given permission
to change

      Not unlike yarrow
      blushing
      in the desert eve,

        each moment

        promising

        fresh colors.
    Saturn,
    and every ring—

You too deserve
wings of sure language
      to draw out
the sweet
dew,

to gather
that wild light
in you. . .

No Wrong Roads Home

Stacie Shannon Denetsosie

In Diné Bizaad, the new disease was called Hatah Nitł'iz, roughly translating to "the body stiffness." But everywhere else called it Scleroceps. The virus originated in North America during the Third World War. The sitting US president was a war-hungry man, quick to declare war on any country that offended him. After losing so many troops to pointless wars, the US military forces were decimated.

After that came the Great Draft, where boys as young as twelve were conscripted and, like broiler chickens, injected with viral vector that triggered the immune response of rapid muscle growth. Boys became the size of men within weeks—growing taller, amassing lean muscle, and recovering faster from fatigue and injury. The news called it the "superhero vaccine." Before lockdown, late at night in my dorm room, I'd watch timelapses of boy soldiers showing off their transformations to trending music. It was a craze at first, people flocking to their doctors requesting the "superhero vaccine," so they could go on spring break shredded, or battle aging's muscle mass loss. But the vaccine had unexpected results—the viral vector somehow mutated, unable to stop replicating.

Those who'd been injected experienced unchecked tissue growth that calcified their muscles and welded their joints in place. The first set of soldiers to be injected became sitting ducks on the battlefield.

"I've never seen anything like it," my mother said to me from the kitchen one evening. She was elbows deep in the sink, hand washing the bowls we'd used for dinner. The news droned on from the living room pinewood entertainment center carved with the infamous Navajo step patterns.

We watched the aerial footage together, troops frozen in position like the terracotta army, unable to move or fight. The opposition annihilated them.

You'd think the story would end there with those troops, but it didn't. Because some of those soldiers were asymptomatic, their muscles didn't seize or lock up, they were able to escape with their lives. And they came home, kissing their partners, visiting their friends, all the while infecting their loved ones with the mutated virus through kisses, shared drinks, and coughs on the bus.

The infection spread from there, at first hardening victims and ravaging their bodies with muscle spasms so painful that the infected would beg for death through their locked jaws. At first, the CDC said that Scleroceps only affected the muscles, but only later was it revealed that in some cases the virus could also impact the frontal lobe, promoting violence and aggression.

After that, all hell broke loose, people attacking their family members, strangers, pets. I bore witness to the Scleroceps virus's power as the case count tripled in my home county the span of three days. That's when I realized that *fear* and *power* could be synonymous.

Scleroceps invaded the Navajo Nation through a Christian revival camp that my mother's patient attended; then my mother fell ill. The disease wreaked havoc on her body; we watched as her body stiffened by the hour, and the Kayenta clinic didn't have the capacity to care for her. She was life-flighted to Phoenix where she was injected with medicines and filled with the meek breath of modern medicine. *Focus on school*, Daddy admonished. *She's a marathon runner—she'll recover.* I did as told. I kept attending classes at my community college in Utah and waited for phone calls from Daddy. Neither of us was prepared to lose her.

Instead of going home, I watched over spotty FaceTime

reception as Daddy propped up his busted iPhone on the hood of his patrol car and put Mama to rest right next to Grandpa in the Kayenta Cemetery. Later that week my Daddy texted me, "*It's getting bad out here.*"

But I could tell by the fresh burial mounds, and we read the same headlines.

Two new deaths

101 additional Scleroceps Virus cases reported on the Navajo Nation—The largest jump in one day

Scleroceps virus could wipe out Indigenous Peoples

The Navajo Nation one of the biggest hotspots for Scleroceps virus in the US

President of Navajo Nation announces lockdown and enforces strict curfews with $1,000 fines.

I spent days in lockdown, my door deadbolted, as advised by our community college, because you never knew who caught the rage strain of the virus. I recalled nights, huddled in my bed as someone infected with the rage pounded on all the doors in our apartment complex, demanding to be let in, until campus security sedated them. During those long nights, I kicked my air purifier up a notch and prayed using the little corn pollen I had left from my mother before she passed.

Desperate for connection, I turned to AI, hoping it could predict the future. I'd glare into the glass screen of my cell phone seeing the same answers for infection mitigation that I'd seen everywhere else: wear a mask, social distance, sanitize often. How was it that since the last two pandemics that masking was the most advanced technology, we could do to avoid getting Scleroceps? Like, wasn't that the same method we used during the 1918 flu? How had there been no technological advances since then? The country could inject our military with a muscle mass inducing vaccine, but couldn't figure out how to keep the vulnerable safe?

These days Daddy called right after he got off night patrol. Since Daddy was a tribal officer on the Navajo Nation, he was called to enforce NN President's curfew. This morning, he called me at six in the morning, two hours later than usual.

"Kiana? Kiana?" He said my name urgently, worried as to why I hadn't responded.

"Hi, Dad."

"How are your classes going?" He asked this as a roundabout way to gauge how I was doing. I was thankful we were not on FaceTime. I didn't want him to see the ants crawling all over my uneaten boxed meal plan lunches, my unwashed hair, or my raw salt-coarse cheeks.

"Everything is online now," I sighed. "Good news is that I can do PE from bed, if my camera is off."

"She would have wanted you to do well in school, mágí." Daddy had taken to the phrase *she would have wanted you to* as if Mama explicitly told him this in life or communicated this with him from the great beyond.

"I miss her."

"I do too." Daddy yawned a great aching yawn, one that expressed that he, like me, suffered from insomnia after our shared loss. His yawn was contagious. I yawned back at him, as if to say, *we are both suffering.*

"Okay, Daddio, I gotta go to class."

"Take care, Ky."

Click.

I never planned on attending my online lecture—my professor recorded them—and I liked to save those for those 2 a.m. when social media couldn't keep the grief at bay, and I needed a droning voice to send me to sleep. Instead, I crawled back into bed and had just started drifting off when my phone chimed.

Taro: u still in bed?

Kiana: yessir, it's early

I tapped out on my keyboard. Before I'd even hit send, Taro's message came in.

Taro: come skating with me in the parking lot

Kiana: im okay. i have lectures to catch up on.

Taro: when's the last time you left your room?

Kiana: idk a week or so

Taro: more like two. cmon, it's just skating.
we can social distance. 😉

Before I could say more, there was rap at my bedroom window. I pulled up my bedroom blinds that sent a flurry of dust into the air, my air purifier momentarily kicked on higher. Taro flashed a bright smile and waved his long board at me, through the crack in the blinds. I rolled my eyes, dropping the blinds. Taro rapped on the window again, this time wearing a mask, and motioning to it, as if to say—now you have no excuse. Sighing, I turned to my dresser and pulled a new mask out from my sock drawer.

Taro was a year older than me. We attended the same high school but didn't hang out in the same crowds. He was friends with my maternal cousin. Sometimes he'd come over to play video games at my auntie's house. Unlike my cousin's other friends, Taro helped with chores, offered to chop wood, rake the yard, and help wash up after a meal. He was taller, more angular. He'd grown into his stocky body. The roundness of boyhood had redistributed into muscle along his arms and legs. When the war was first declared, Taro was ready and willing to serve his country, his bull riding rodeo club days gave him one too many concussions and he was deemed unfit for the military. It broke his heart to watch my cousin go into the field without him.

"Been reading the news?" I asked. Taro squatted down next to me on the curb. His shins dawned purple since he'd taken up skateboarding as a regular hobby.

"Heeelll naw," he said. "If I want to want to be depressed, I just call my mom." Taro's eyes crinkled with a wince behind his mask.

"My mom was like that too," I said.

"Look, I didn't mean that I'm sorry I said it like that. I meant to say, my mom is dramatic—Fuck—I can't say the right thing." Taro dropped his head into his hands, ruffling his black moplike hair.

"There's no right thing to say," I sighed.

Taro paused.

"Then I won't say anything." He sucked in a deep breath. "How about we leave town this week? My mom, she's running low on some necessities. Bashas' ran out of toilet paper and my mom's flipping her lid."

My eyes widened. "We could start at Clark's!"

"You really haven't left your dorm lately, have you? They're straight up empty. Nothing. Nada."

"Well, what about Cortez? Or we could just shoot to Farmington," I suggested.

"Every John is going to Cortez and Farmington," he said, and I nodded in agreement. "The stores are price gouging Natives who drive three damn hours to get there. I say we go north toward Salt Lake and hit up the nearest Walmart."

We decided to meet back up in the parking lot after we pack up our things. Taro and I both packed light because we'd need as much of his Ford Ranger's bed for supplies as possible. Taro's truck was equipped with a locking camper shell. Taro opened the camper and tailgate to load my backpack and said, "Apparently, the dorm bed fits perfectly in the bed of the truck."

I rolled my eyes at him, but secretly I was thankful for the bed. A part of me hoped that we wouldn't have to use it, and that we'd be so invigorated after shopping we'd just speed home without sleep. Another small part of me imagined us sealed in the camper as close as sardines and a small part of me hungered for it, to feel Taro's breath wash over my face and taste the pink of his inner lip.

My heart pinched with guilt imagining this. I hadn't even been in the same room as another human since my mother passed from fear of contracting the virus. I stayed holed up in my room, washing my hands so frequently that my hands cracked and bled, and microwaving my food to ensure that everything would be killed. How could I imagine even touching Taro, if I couldn't eat a cold cut sandwich unless it'd been adequately nuked for at least three minutes? What was romance supposed to look like during a pandemic? These were the kinds of questions I used to take to my mother, who always knew how to calm me down and stop me from jumping to conclusions. Without her, the world felt overwhelming—too vast, too contagious. I would've done anything to help her, so helping Taro help his mom felt like the next best thing, health risks be damned.

Taro jumped into the front seat and started up his Ranger. An outdated *Navajo Tribal Utility Authority* dash calendar fluttered on the dashboard. Surface wise, his truck was a mess, red sand filling every crevice, tiny pebbles littering the floor mats, and windows tinted so darkly that the world outside his truck appeared sepia.

As we started north, the roads were filled with trucks and trailers heading toward Moab. Folks were taking quarantine as an opportunity to camp or go on vacation. If they were headed to Lake Powell, they'd have to drive through my reservation. They'd touch our gas pumps and infect our people—without knowing it, whether they were asymptomatic or not. Either way, my people would pay the price.

Taro and I were silent for a couple of hours, neither of us

saying anything. I'd been on road trips before with boys who'd say nothing until we got to our destination. It was different from when I traveled with my girlfriends, and we'd hit up Page to go to the movies or walk around the mall. We'd laugh and gossip the whole way there, talking about which boys in our classes were the cutest, teasing Cora for sleeping with her red-headed boyfriend, and singing to our favorite nostalgic songs. I thought boys were more serious. They seemed more destination-minded, and everything was far less fun. I thought of my parents, my mother standing on the side of the highway in PPE testing the mile-long road of men, women, elders, and children with long cotton swabs, the technology on the reservation largely disparate compared to the rest of the country's AI Nero-brain scanners. How often did she run to another line to translate for another nurse, when an elder only spoke Navajo? How hot was it outside? Would her nose get a rash from her face mask, like the pictures I'd seen of doctors on the news? I thought of my father, the blare of the horn that rung through our hometown at curfew, and I imagined him patrolling our hometown with his spotlight at night. Last we talked, he'd given out several thousand-dollar fines, and he oversaw making sure that only critical workers were allowed in and out of town.

"You know what? We're so close to it, but I've never been to Moab," I said, as we passed the welcome sign. "I've always thought that vacationing in Moab was like a rich bilagáana thing, like I don't see any Navajos leaving the rez to go Jeeping or mountain biking in Moab, maybe because all that shit's in our own backyard. It's still pretty though."

I pressed my masked nose up against the windshield looking up at the vermillion cliffs streaked with white, where the iron-oxide had leached way.

Moab was a pretty town complete with an Indian Trading Post with windows that felt like you were looking into a case of fine turquoise jewelry. Kokopelli seemed to be stamped on the side of nearly every building. One restaurant flaunted a giant torch outside their eatery so bright and orange, that I was nearly enticed to find out what *EL FUEGO*'s weekly special was. Several Jeeps passed us filled with young attractive white teenagers, girls in midriff-baring crop tops and gift shop cowboy hats, and the boys sporting tousled surfer hair and bronze freckled shoulders.

That's about when Taro called for a piss break.

"Wanna know something funny?" Taro asked. The sunset glinted off his slick black eyelashes.

I nodded.

"This end-of-the-world shit. I think it's funny, cuz, like, we've already lived through it, you know?" he said, smiling. "Like our ancestors. They lived through the diseases that Anglos brought to this continent and the 1918 flu. It's like we've been living in that one movie, *I Am Legend*, since they've come here. It's always been bad. Like right now, we have to drive hours to go to a Walmart to get supplies. We drive trucks because rez roads are shit. And when you're Navajo, you can't trust no one." He paused, searching my eyes for any hint of judgment at his rez accent, then continued, "I mean—anyone. Except for this time, we *actually* have to worry about getting infected."

He was right. All Natives have lived in a dystopia since colonization. We're the rebel band with burning sage and bandanas over our mouths.

Three hours later, we'd hit Price and pulled into the Walmart parking lot. Taro stepped out of the car, switched out his mask for a fresh one, and then covered his mask with a red bandana.

"There's another bandana in the glove box," he said.

Reaching in, I pulled out a matching bandana and tied it around my face. We secured a cart and I wiped it down with the complimentary alcohol wipe offered at the door.

A wave of air rushed over us as we entered the store. Taro walked over to the carts and pulled one out for us. I followed his lead and pulled out my own. We'd have to do double the shopping.

"What's on your list?" he asked.

I looked down at my phone.

"Potatoes, Spam, corned beef, flour…"

In the produce aisle, a printed sign read they were limiting potato purchases to one bag per customer.

"We'll do two transactions, and then we'll come back in to do another," Taro said. I nodded and grabbed two bags of potatoes; they felt light in my arms as I placed them in the cart. We continued through the rest of the store like that, reading the printed memos.

Limit one pack of paper towels per household.

We'd take two.

The cleaning aisle was wiped clean, except for some stray gallons of bleach. I grabbed two gallons of bleach, in case my grandma would have to sanitize her own water in a worst-case scenario. Next, we picked up several cases of Carnation milk, in case my grandmother had lambs and could not buy lamb formula. As our load grew, so did the looks of bewilderment. Folks stared at us. Who are these two Navajos taking all of *our* groceries? By the time we were done, we swiped nearly three huundred dollars of nonperishables onto my college credit card.

We took this load out to the truck and unloaded everything into the camper. I stacked as many cans of food as I could in the cab of the truck and then moved on into the truck bed. Taro lay on the mattress on his stomach carefully arranging cans around the edges of the bed.

"We should head north to another Walmart and then on the way back we can hit this one up again."

I agreed with him. I didn't want to spend too much time in one store in case someone freaked out and got suspicious.

Taro and I hopped back into the truck and headed another hour and a half north to Spanish Fork, where there are several Walmarts in a twenty-minute radius.

"How do you know your way around so well?" I asked as Taro effortlessly merged onto the highway and navigated to a nearby exit.

"I used to work up this way with my brother. Yeah, after graduation, I thought I wanted to be a welder because of that college trade program we had in high school, so I moved in with my aunt who lived up North and worked at a welding shop. The pay was shitty and the boss was mean. Me and Ricky, we sucked it up for a year, working for that angry old man. We were just working for our mom. We'd get paid and send our paychecks home to her." Taro smiled a little.

A lot of moms did that back at home. They'd send their sons off and ask them for money, using it to buy new purses, and finance new trucks.

"That's not fair," I said.

Taro shot an accusatory look at me.

"My dad passed on when we were little kids. It's always just been me and my brother and our mom. She went through hell and still raised us. It's the least we could do." Taro straightened his hands on the steering wheel and casting his eyes out onto the freeway.

"Whoa, I'm sorry."

"Don't be sorry if you mean what you say," Taro said, tightening his jaw.

"Sorry, Taro. I didn't know."

"How could you know, your mom was a nurse and your dad's a cop? You don't know what it's like to run out of food stamp money or wear wrong sized shoes to school, just so your mom doesn't feel guilty that she's not bringing enough home!"

His words stung like hand sanitizer on an unseen cut.

The truck went silent for a few minutes, the whine of the

engine whirring through the cabin. Shutting my eyes, I fought the warmth accumulating there. As I inhaled, Taro's rough hand met mine, giving it a gentle squeeze. Instead of squeezing back, I flinched and pulled away.

"Please," I said through my teeth, "—don't touch me."

Panic rose in my chest as I groped for my purse on the floor. I fished out the hand sanitizer, squeezed out a quarter-sized glob, and worked it into my hands until every crack in my hand sang with pain, until my wrists and forearms smelled like artificial lemons. I didn't dare look at Taro, not even my father knew how bad my mysophobia had gotten.

When we arrived at the second store Taro, and I were no longer in sync. I left him at the truck, rushing into the store before he was ready. I loaded trays of cans into my cart. Some staples for the animals, wet cat food, a bag of dog food.

Before I left the aisle, Taro met me halfway, between the catnip and flea collars.

Maintaining eye contact, he shoveled a couple dozen cans of wet dog food into his cart. The cans crashed into the cart.

"Stop, you'll get us in trouble," I growled.

"I'm going to load groceries my own way, thank you," Taro said, leaning on his cart arms splayed.

"You're going to draw unwanted atten—"

A sudden grunt at the far end of the aisle made us both jump. A man, roughly our age staggered toward us, as if he were being held upright by an unseen rod, his movements sharp and exaggerated. His mouth hung open in that horrifying O so many Scleroceps victims wore.

The spittle accumulating at the corners of his mouth stretching into sticky webs each time it bobbed open and closed, like a fish gasping for air.

My jaw felt sore just looking at him.

Taro stepped away from his cart and toward mine. "This guy is really sick," he said under his breath. The man staggered forward, lunging toward my cart—the only thing between us.

"Whatcha doing off yur reservation little Indians?" he asked, the veins in his neck throbbing, clearly fighting the muscle lock.

Some bystanders glanced in our direction before hurrying away. In my peripheral, I saw a blue vested employee reach for his walkie talkie before fleeing the scene.

"Just picking up groceries for our families," Taro responded, taking a defensive step back.

"Don'tcha already get enough handouts from the government?" The man yanked the cart out of my hands.

"No sir, our grocery stores are empty," I stammered.

"Liar!" he yelled, white knuckling my cart before slamming into my stomach.

The air knocked from my lungs with a solid woosh. I fell to the floor, the man hulking over me with my cart.

"Better teach ya kids a lesson about stealing what doesn't belong to you!"

Out of nowhere, Taro barreled into the man's chest, his car keys clattering to the floor. The man fell sidelong into the shelf, toppling it with a huge crash. Dog food cans scattered across the floor, a stray can rolled and hit my foot.

Taro had the man in a headlock, his brown arms straining around the thick bands of the man's neck. His headlock arm shaking, as the man pulled own on his elbow. He was too strong for Taro. The man groped backward reaching for Taro's head, getting a fistful of black hair.

"Imma going to wring your neck," the man howled.

Taro was losing purchase on the man. My heart thudded in my chest. The man was balmy with the deathly sheen of Scleroceps, he was a walking infection, and if I didn't do anything he was going to kill Taro. I crawled for Taro's keys, taking the Ford Ranger's switch blade like key in-between my fingers, and dived into the man, plunging it deep into his eyeball which gave way with a sickening pop.

The aftermath of the attack was overwhelming. A group of medical professionals in hazmat suits cleaned up the man's body and threw us into a van where they hosed us down with hospital grade cleaners. After the attack, I sat with a wool blanket wrapped around my shoulders in Taro's camper. We'd left the Walmart and had parked for the night in Spanish Fork Canyon. I'd lost my last mask in the fight.

The sun was setting, bathing the canyon in a reddish glow, the color of the hot cinnamon lollypops my mother liked so much.

Taro joined me on the tailgate of the camper for a moment.

"That's really pretty," he said looking at me.

I hid my smile behind the blanket.

"It's a shame that you hide your smile like that."

Nervous energy extended between us. To break the awkwardness, he flopped into the truck bed like a centipede crawling under a rock. He pushed white grocery bags into the recesses of the wheel well and stacked the cans of Spam against the sides of the truck.

"It should be good for sleeping now." His voice sounded distant, as if emanating from deep within a cave. He crawled back out, his black Vans first then his legs.

"You can sleep in here and I'll sleep in the cab," he said, thumbing over his shoulder.

"That can't be comfortable." I felt the hair on my legs prickle in the mountain breeze.

"The seat reclines...a little bit...I've done it before." Taro palmed the back of his neck.

"Okay, if you say so," I said, chucking my blanket into the back of the camper trailer, my volleyball shorts slick against the bare mattress.

Taro shut the tail gate. He started to shut the camper visor, but before he could, I stopped him.

"Wait, I think that there's enough room in here for two people." I feel every part of myself prepare for rejection.

Taro tilted his head back and frowns. "So, you yell at me in Walmart, save my life, and now you want to sleep with me?"

"No, ew! I don't want to sleep with you. I just think it would be more comfortable if you slept back here too. That way you could stretch out and get a good night's sleep."

"You know what, Kiana, I don't get you. You're all somehow one second, and then the next you *try* to be nice. It's confusing and I don't get it." Taro stepped back.

"Please, Taro, I don't want to sleep in here alone. I'm scared. I miss my family and I'm just having a hard time."

"Fine." Taro climbed into the back of the truck and shuts the camper visor.

I scooted to the left side of the truck bed, my head close to a stack of Spam tins.

Taro lay down, cradling his head with his arm.

I lay down beside him. He turned ever so slightly and wrapped his arm around me. We were there like that for a long while. My wool blanket pulled up over my shoulder.

"I can see your face you know," he said in the dark, "and I can tell that you love this." He chuckled under his breath.

"Don't flatter yourself," I said.

Taro drew his arms around me, and I fell asleep listening to the even rhythm of his breath and the whistle of the wind through the camper windows.

When we cross the Navajo Nation border, my dad is there in his pickup truck. Police lights flash onto the nearby Mesa and pulse through the desert. The stars are out. It would be a beautiful night to sleep outside in my grandma's shade house, where we'd peek through the wood slat roof and name constellations. Taro and I jump out of the car and open the trunk. The bags are stacked on top of each other on the mattress piled on top of each other, touching the top of the camper's fiberglass ceiling, like little white eggs in a spider's nest.

My dad knows the officer on patrol, and Taro helps him unload the truck, careful not to bump into him. He keeps his eyes down, like he did when he used to visit my aunt's house.

"Kiana, shí yazhí, thank you," my father says as we unload the last of groceries. He looks at me, the white, and blue flashing lights flickering off his eyes like a hot flame. He's seen the mattress, and I want to tell him nothing happened, that Taro just slept in the cab of the truck. I want to say something that keeps me younger, like a child, his child in this moment—but we both know that something within me has shifted. That I'm no longer the child that screams out at night because a moth is hitting my bedroom window, that in my own right, I've become a provider. But we just stare at each other, across the tar-latticed reservation road.

A Lesson in Love and Insanity

Arielle Twist

My father always told us that the definition of insanity
is doing the exact same thing over and over again,
hoping for a different outcome

The ants have started to show up on the counter
I spray them with Lysol, wipe them off with a paper towel
and
in the mundanity of this act, there you are
standing half asleep, arms stretched
asking to be held
I oblige and though
I say that like I don't want to
I promise it's all I want in the moment
please forgive my passiveness
my indifference is out of self-preservation
or this is what I am learning about myself
as I have tried this many times before
but not with you
and here we are in that kitchen and
I don't know that you'll remember
the moments when you're half asleep
wandering into a room like a kid waking up
in the middle of the night looking for their mum
wanting to be held, to be loved
It's so hard to not give you all of me
to not let you change me into whatever
you need me to be because I can be

I can try at least

It may seem like madness to want to love after all this
I have shared my heartbreaks with the world
thinking that healing would accompany
vocalizing the trope that is a trans life
I can recall the first day he made me feel like
there was something in me worth more
without the burden of being a god
that I don't have to try
and
here I am
still full of hope
for a different outcome

Exilio

Maritza N. Estrada

We are exiles, I tell you. Exilados.
and it has been so long, long in point; return.
There. Over there. One year turns to one hundred
years, far from home, root, or tomb.
Passing turns: that's how it goes.

Mo-ver.

As if I just may be closer to *there*—
bow head every land traveled: access / denied.
Ma'am, please present identification. and if not
in proper position, pose, or point of eye
contact walk as if a machete's tip prepares to kiss
the S-curve of spine all the way down until halved.

There, the people of Guerrero
point prayer, counting each rosary bead
like each llanto matters. Every fallen head
sits like stone, decayed dates under sol burning.
En cansancio lamento. *Puedes pasar este mensaje
a mi familia*, a voice asks. Nod, though you know
in passing line the message won't reach the beloved.
In a bus, reach hand to window of the land's carrying
in what I take of it, from, to another country.
The city people fear us from the mountains, a prima blesses
in parting.

Nos vemos.

There—you see
the mountains of Washington
are no different of Guerrero.
Of guerra comes a silent war
language: this body is war inheritance.

Everywhere, there—a stranger hands
me a machete, book, or kiss.
                    Remember me.

                    Are you in faith of your
                    country, land, inheritance?

Do let me answer. Not until then. Here.

The Stolen Drawing

Conley Lyons

Josephine Morningstar had worked on that colored pencil drawing for three whole weeks, and now it was gone.

It wasn't an ordinary drawing either, no matter what stupid Damian Whitefeather said. Miss Houston, the art teacher for their sixth-grade class on Tuesdays, Wednesdays, and every other Friday, had asked them all to draw an *optical illusion* for this unit.

Josephine had never heard those words before. But after Miss Houston explained, she thought she understood the idea pretty well. You were supposed to draw something that was there but not there at the exact same time. Kind of like when her family sat out in the backyard in summer with the sprinkler running and a little rainbow sparkled through the mist and through the side of her dad's empty beer glass. The rainbow didn't live inside the glass but showed up now and then if you looked at the curved lip the right way, in the right light.

Anyhow, she spent hours and hours hunched over a piece of thick white paper as wide as her desk, rubbing her pink eraser over the big crooked black lines streaking down the middle of the page till the eraser shed little rubber pieces all over. Carefully shading the middle of the water with blues and greens and golds and corals. She told Miss Houston that she wanted her drawing to feel like a person seeing everyday things in a fishbowl of water. She'd even taken a photo of some stuff in the bottom of a mixing bowl as a *reference*, another art term she'd learned in class. The photo showed a bunch of hidden objects under a wavy layer of water: holographic hairclips, push pins, cool erasers, and a broken CD she found stuffed in the back of the TV stand. Shimmery things that would be fun to draw.

Taking the photos on Monty's phone and printing them out at the library also cost her four whole dollars because that's how much he wanted for stupid Robux in exchange. Monty had an Xbox and could buy extra things for his idiot Roblox games when Mom wouldn't even let Josephine have a real phone yet.

After all that—after she'd spent weeks trying to make her drawing perfect and even longer imagining how pretty it would look tacked up on the showcase bulletin board between the art room and the cafeteria hallway—it was gone.

"I'm gonna figure out who did this," she told her best friend Cressida Greywolf at recess between messy sniffles. "It's an *injustice.*"

They were sitting at the far corner of the playground, on a long wooden beam marking where the mulch stopped and the grassy field beyond the school began. Josephine's sadness was weighing her down now, heavier than an old backpack stuffed full of textbooks. This morning, she'd started out being really brave about having the fishbowl stolen, but now she was swiping big fat tears away from her eyes with the corner of her sweatshirt sleeve.

Cressida had been Josephine's best friend all the way since second grade, when they got assigned desks next to each other and spent the whole year getting in trouble for talking. She was a great best friend, funny and kind, and never mentioning the way Josephine got hot-tempered about what her mom called the silliest things. "Like, I better not see Brayden Coffey stuffing it in his backpack later, or it's *on.* I will open the slap box. No cap. He'll get got!"

Josephine gave a watery laugh. Cressida always knew how to make her feel better. Although she was starting to think she'd said the wrong word before. Mom always said she got kind of dramatic when she was depressed. "Maybe it's not, like, actual injustice."

Not like the stories she'd heard from her parents and grand-parents when she was little.

Cressida looked thoughtful. Her dark curly hair puffed out behind her like cotton candy and bright dentalium earrings gleamed in both ears. Probably her mom's. "Well, it could be a tiny one. Like when that weird old man took my grandma's good planter off her front porch."

Josephine remembered that story. Hard to forget. Cressida's grandma Ellie was almost eighty, but after a million years of farm work, she could probably still punch somebody's lights out if they messed around with her. Her shoulders were wider than Monty's. "Didn't she also tell that guy that if he didn't give it back, she was gonna shoot out his front tires?"

"Yeah, she did say that. And she would've. Only it was back by supper."

Josephine muffled a giggle in her sweatshirt. Ellie was the best.

"Anyway," Cressida said, as they watched two boys streak through the thin mulch a few feet away, a blue Frisbee soaring over their heads, "I think you have to go around and ask other people what they saw before you do anything too crazy."

"I already told my homeroom teacher it was missing." Mrs. Robin had also given her a narrow-eyed, disappointed look when Josephine told her what had happened. It was the kind of look that usually came before some kind of quiet lecture, like, *whining about grades won't do any good or I think you need to solve your own problems.* "She said to go ask Miss Houston."

"So did you go?" Cressida asked.

"Not yet." Josephine dug the toe of one scuffed sneaker into the mulch. They were greyish and too big for her because they'd been Monty's shoes, first. "She's here today, though. Let's see if we can go at lunch."

As Josephine and Cressida opened the door to Miss Houston's room, they expected Miss Houston to be standing at the front of the classroom like usual, wearing her big colorful dress and funky glasses. Instead, an almost-empty room greeted them. The only difference was that a boy they knew stared back at them from one of the middle desk clusters instead. Judging by the scattered paint cans and fistfuls of brushes, he was clearly working on an art project.

Josephine found her voice first. "Joshy Merriwether?"

Joshy was actually named Josh Junior, but not even his parents called him that. The only people who ever said Josh Junior were teachers reading roll call on the first day of school. Josephine didn't know much about him, other than that he had two sisters, his dad (Big Josh) was a fancy nurse at the hospital, and the family had a pet rabbit named Bunnicula.

He looked confused to see them, too. The sides of his baggy John Cena T-shirt rippled in the breeze from the open door. A few wispy pieces of hair hung loose from his braid, waving around his face. "Why aren't you guys at lunch?"

Josephine glanced around the art room. The endless quiet gave her an eerie feeling. Miss Houston's desk just had her computer monitor, piles of paper, and some notebooks sitting on it. She didn't think kids were even allowed to skip lunch to hang out in empty classrooms. "Why aren't you?"

He pointed to his work table. A big half-finished canvas, still wet, was surrounded by paints and brushes on one side, while his open lunchbox sat on the other. Josephine could see an empty Ziploc bag sticking out of it. "I have to go to the dentist later. But Miss Houston said I could paint here as long as I cleaned everything up after."

"Oh, really? Is she around?" Cressida folded her arms over her chest like she didn't believe any of this.

"She went to the lounge to get more coffee, I think." Joshy rubbed a smear of dry paint off his arm. "Do y'all have to go to the dentist today, too?"

Josephine sighed.

Although she didn't look at Cressida to see if telling him the truth was a good idea, she wanted to. It felt important to talk about it, especially to someone else who cared about making good art. If he was down here painting during lunch, then he wasn't just trying to coast through for no reason. "Somebody took my showcase drawing. We think."

"Oh man. The fishbowl?" Joshy's mouth fell open. "That sucks. Those colors looked so good."

Josephine nodded. Her face got hot again like she might cry. "Yeah."

"Do you know who did it?"

"She wishes," Cressida jumped in. "We were hoping Miss Houston was here to ask."

Joshy pushed hair from his face, pursing his mouth like this was giving him a lot of new ideas. "Huh. Well, when did you find out it was missing?"

Josephine took a steadying breath. "This morning. I came by to see when the showcase was going up. Miss Houston put all our packets from this unit in the plastic box outside her door, like she always does."

All the artwork was collected in a file folder with their names on the front. Each folder was held together by a big paper clip, the thick black kind with silver wings that looked like a folded dragonfly. Miss Houston usually put projects out in the mornings before class started.

"And your packet was there with your other drawings?"

Josephine nodded. Everything else had been exactly as she remembered it.

"Hmm." He was brushing one palm over the top of a clean paintbrush. Josephine watched as its bristles zipped backward and forward like corn waving in a field. "Could have been an accident. Can you think of anyone with a good motive for taking it?"

It was a smart question. Until now, Josephine hadn't really considered that someone would take it on purpose. Or hadn't wanted to think that, maybe.

But Cressida hooted out a laugh. "Oh my god. Motive? Who *says* that?!"

Joshy didn't smile. He had always been pretty serious in class, but now he looked like he was ready to go to a funeral. "My dad streams a lot of detective shows. They always say there has to be a reason behind every crime. That's motive."

"It's not a crime," Josephine said loudly, even though her chest tightened with sadness as she thought about someone taking her drawing on purpose. "It just sucks."

"Okay." Joshy barely blinked as he exchanged the paintbrush for a stubby No. 2 pencil, now twirling it around his index and middle fingers. "So who do you think would have taken it?"

Josephine thought about this, but before she could answer, high heels clicked down the long hallway, getting louder with each step. Miss Houston was probably coming back from the teacher's lounge. They wouldn't be able to talk for real if a teacher was around. "Maybe we can ask some kids this afternoon, once school's out. When's your dentist appointment?"

"One thirty. And then my dad's dropping us back here for basketball practice, after."

"Cool." Cressida said. "So you'll help us talk to whoever we see in the gym?"

Joshy looked surprised to be asked, but he stuck his pencil behind one ear like they'd just told him to figure out a solution to climate change. "Sure. I'll be there."

✦

By three-fifteen, Josephine had finished her social studies and English homework and had met up with Joshy and Cressida. Apart from the silver filling IHS had put in his back tooth, which he gleefully showed her after she asked, he was fine.

"So," Josephine said, scanning the bleachers. The basketball players were doing warm-up drills across half-court, and everyone who wasn't part of practice sat in the stands with their backpacks and lunchboxes in small groups of twos and threes. "We should talk to Brayden Coffey soon, since his mom usually picks him up by four."

"He'll get got," Cressida muttered under her breath.

"I really don't think it was him, Cress." Brayden didn't like her, but he also didn't care about art. He'd gotten so many points for misbehaving that they'd moved him to metal shop right after the midterm. Probably after he stabbed George Miers in the forearm with a pencil. Which was an accident. They hoped. "If he wanted to be mean to me, he'd just call me a bucktoothed beeyotch again."

"Or shove you into a wall, maybe," Joshy said.

Josephine didn't want to know how Joshy knew that. Monty always said a lot of crap went down in the boys' locker rooms when nobody was watching. "Right."

Her heartbeat sped up at the idea of trying to ask Brayden anything. He was the meanest kid in their grade and had been since they were practically babies. She shivered at the idea of having his full attention. "Maybe we talk to other kids from art, first?"

They started with Diana Hawk, a broad, sturdy girl with sun-browned arms who'd been at Medicine Park Elementary since kindergarten. She sat at the table next to Josephine's with a couple other seventh-graders from track. She liked working with charcoal and was learning how to throw shot put.

"Let me look through my packet," she said, after Josephine explained the situation. "Maybe it just got put in the wrong folder."

That was easier to think about than someone taking it on purpose.

Diana searched for a minute. Josephine saw several charcoal pieces and a couple of black and white still lifes, but no fishbowl. She swore under her breath.

"Sorry." Diana pointed down the bleachers. "Try Kayleigh Grace?"

Kayleigh Grace was a sprinter who always wore her bright blonde hair in two high ponytails topped with beaded barrettes. She looked through her folder too, but it only had acrylic paintings of unicorns and fantasy creatures.

They talked to Kayleigh's friend Becka March, a guitar player, then four sporty girls from the basketball team, then a table full of gangly long-haired Shoshone boys who were new to Medicine Park, but who Joshy told her were really into deer hunting and X-Men.

Nothing.

"God," Cressida groaned, after they'd finished talking to the X-boys. She'd fished out her phone from her backpack to take a quick point-five of them on the bleachers before tossing the phone back into her bag. "This is so annoyyying. I just want to slap whoever did it!"

"Don't worry, Josephine." Joshy put a hand on her elbow. "On TV they never solve anything until later in the show."

Mr. Shipman, standing by the back doors, waved to get their attention. "Hey, Jo! Number 181 is right around the corner. Let's be ready, huh?"

That meant her mom was almost here and Josephine would have to grab her stuff fast.

"Okay," Josephine called back.

She turned to Joshy and Cressida, letting out a big sigh. "I gotta go. Let's meet back up tomorrow."

✦

They weren't able to see each other again until lunch the next day. Joshy turned out to have the same lunch as Josephine, even though she was coming from science and he had English.

"Okay." Joshy consulted a handwritten list on a piece of notebook paper, checking off names as he went. Josephine hadn't seen anyone except old people do that. "So I talked to the rest of the basketball girls, plus the nerdy goth dudes into tabletop gaming. None of them had the fishbowl or saw it after we turned in our projects for the showcase."

Josephine didn't think Joshy had any business calling anyone nerdy, considering he had a lightsaber lunchbox and was wearing a shirt with Han Solo on it. But she kept that to herself. "I asked Ms. Race and Mr. Suarez if they'd seen anything, too. They just told me they'd keep their eyes open. Whatever that means."

"Well." Joshy scratched their names onto his list with his stubby pencil. "Guess it's better than nothing."

"And I think Cress is asking Mrs. Pitt if she's seen it after Pre-Algebra gets out. So that just leaves...."

They glanced over to the long grey table by the window where the six most popular kids in second lunch sat: Cherry Roman, the Beaulieu twins, Damian Whitefeather, Brayden Coffey, and Riley Jane Mercer, Brayden's girlfriend.

"We don't have to go over there right now," Joshy said.

Josephine's stomach cramped with nerves, but she ignored it. Even if Brayden wasn't in art anymore, Cherry and Riley were and maybe they had seen what happened to the fishbowl. It was probably the best thing she'd ever drawn. She'd never be able to forgive herself if she didn't ask them about it. "I just want to get it over with. Come on."

Taking a deep breath, she got up from the plastic seat, trying to ignore how the back of her thighs had stuck to it in the September heat. During second lunch, the cafeteria was always full: kids waiting to file through the lunch line with trays and coming out with rectangular pizza or a bowl of fries; kids trading chips and cookies and sandwiches from shapeless lunch bags; the teacher on duty lurking around the doors with a big smoothie cup and dark smudges under their eyes.

As she walked closer, she could start to pick out some of their conversation over the roar of the room.

"You still listening to Meek Mill?" Damian had a thicker accent, making the word *Mill* sound like meal.

"Why?" Brayden's voice was higher, kind of nasal.

Damian laughed so loudly the echo clapped around the walls. "Just asking questions, dummy! God."

Brayden didn't seem to care. One side of his mouth turned up in a smile as he leaned toward Riley who was sitting between him and one of the twins. "Bro heard three Kendrick songs and thinks he's god of rizz."

The entire table cracked up as one of the Beaulieu twins called out: "Mustaaaaaard!!"

Josephine was now close enough to reach out and touch the end of their table with her fingertips. She took a deep breath. "Hey, guys?"

Nothing. They were so busy laughing they didn't even look over.

She wet her lips with the tip of her tongue and straightened her spine. "Hey."

She could hear Monty's voice in her head all of a sudden like he was standing right behind her instead of sitting in class on the other side of the county. *Look them dead in the eye! Take up space! You're a Morningstar, and you're almost twelve, so quit that scared baby stuff and act like it!*

"Hey!" she said loudly.

Six heads turned in her direction.

"Cherry. Riley. I'm trying to find out what happened to my pencil drawing from this quarter. The, um, fishbowl?" Josephine's palms were sweating; she rubbed them on the sides of her shorts. "It's supposed to go in the showcase, but no one knows where it is. You haven't seen it anywhere, have you?"

"No," said Cherry, pursing glossy lips. "Sorry."

"Man, why the hell would we know anything about that?" Damian asked. Both corners of his mouth were turning up.

Josephine didn't smile. "I don't know."

"Negative rizz," Brayden murmured to Riley, loud enough that the Beaulieu twins giggled.

"Okay, do you know where it is, then?" Josephine asked him directly.

"Not in art anymore, dumbass. And I'm glad. Miss Houston's a bitch, plus it's full of losers."

"Well, you sucked at it anyway," Josephine said, as her entire body flooded with heat. "What's that say about you?"

Brayden fixed her with a look that could have frozen ice. "Least my only friends at this school aren't a nerdy fag and an ugly slut whose mom's a stripper."

Beside him, Riley's nostrils flared. She hadn't laughed at Brayden's dumb jokes before, but now she looked pissed off. "Bray."

Josephine should have said something funny and cool in response. Instead, the hot furious feeling took over her entire body, and she socked him in the nose.

Sitting in the nurse's office with the school secretary, Ms. Perry, Josephine decided she wouldn't feel bad, even if she got in more trouble. Even if her mom yelled at her in the car. Punching Brayden in the face was the most badass thing she'd ever done in her whole life, and she wasn't going to waste time being upset about it.

Ms. Perry had just put a Band-Aid on Josephine's index finger when Cressida's head poked around the corner of the doorframe.

"Cressida Greywolf," Ms. Perry said, without looking over. Josephine didn't know how she always seemed to understand what kids were doing before she even had to look at them. "I know you ain't out here missing class when you're two demerits away from losing restroom privileges."

Cressida shook her head, trying to keep from smiling. "Never."

"And I'd never see it happen anyway, since I'm technically waiting for my Lean Cuisine to finish cooking." Ms. Perry fixed Josephine with a stern look that said *don't get up*. "Back in three minutes, Jo."

Once Ms. Perry was gone, Cressida threw her arms around Josephine's neck. Josephine smelled grapefruit and flowers before Cressida pulled away, exclaiming, "Girl, why didn't you wait for me?"

"I wasn't thinking," Josephine said. Which was true. Instead of asking herself whether she should or shouldn't, or if she'd get in trouble, that flash of fury had her lashing out like a copperhead nabbing a field mouse. "Joshy even told me we should wait, but I just wanted to get it over with." She wasn't sure how to admit that she wouldn't have been able to talk to them at all if she'd waited until after school.

Cressida's mouth tightened into a thin line. Very slowly, she took a step backward so that she was standing next to Josephine's shoes instead of right next to her. "You know what? I'm actually tired of hearing about Joshy."

Josephine's body went cold like she'd been sloshed by a giant wave. "What do you mean?"

"We were supposed to be doing this together! You and me, like it's always been. You'd figure out who took it and then I'd go mess that idiot up until they gave it back."

What was she talking about? And since when did Cressida think she had to go around messing people up because Josephine wouldn't? "I don't—"

"Now what? Are you just gonna let some random art kid with a dumbass baby nickname do everything for me, and then I have to hear about the cool drama later? Is that what a best friend does?"

Josephine's eyes pricked with tears. Did she think Josephine wanted Joshy to be her new best friend? She didn't! "Cress. I—"

Cressida glared at her, but there was water shimmering in the bottom of her eyes too. "I have to go."

"Don't!" Josephine called, but Cressida had already moved for the door, the wooden ruler of the bathroom pass dangling awkwardly around her wrist as she disappeared around the doorway.

It was the second time since the fishbowl got stolen that Josephine felt like crying, only this time she put her head down on the bleach- and rubbing alcohol-scented table and let the tears stream down her cheeks, speckling the pale wood.

"Hoooooooly hell, little star." Monty leaned against the door-frame of Josephine's room, folding his arms across his chest. He was trying to make his face all serious, but this was the happiest he'd ever sounded, apart from getting his Xbox for Christmas two years ago. "Can't believe you got in a real fight and they're only giving you three days of lunch detention. Last year, these two country girls in tenth grade got into a knockdown, drag-out brawl before school, and they got OSS for two weeks. Each!"

"Sucks for them," Josephine said dully. She couldn't be bothered to care about some dumbass sophomores right now.

Monty seemed to understand how pissed off she was without asking a lot of questions. "What'd that little dickhead do, anyway? He the one who took your drawing?"

"No." She heaved out a breath. "Said awful stuff about Cress's mom, because she....you know...and he called Joshy...something else."

Monty sniffed like this really wasn't the kind of stuff to go punching anyone over. Maybe once you got to high school you only ever got into fights over boyfriends and girlfriends. "Is Joshy the little gay one? Big Josh's boy?"

"Monty! You're such an idiot!"

Josephine crumpled up a piece of notebook paper and threw paper balls at him for at least a minute before he made the time-out sign with both hands.

"Hey, I didn't mean anything bad by it, J-bird. People just talk, you know?"

"Well, they shouldn't," Josephine said.

From the kitchen, they could hear the slam of pots and pans in the sink. The guilt in Josephine's chest was mixed with some kind of weird pride at being the one in trouble, for once. Some-one had been mean to her and instead of taking it, or running home crying, she'd done something about it.

"Is Mom really mad?" she asked, biting her lip.

She had yelled in the car, but not about Josephine's behav-ior. Mostly about Brayden's parents and how idiotic they were and how their kid was a no-good s-heel who was full of negative energy and was mean to people for effing idiot reasons.

Monty laughed, like Josephine had asked a stupid ques-tion. But when he smiled, he got the kind of deep crinkles around his eyes that said she shouldn't freak out about it too much. "She's just dreaming of ways to kill that principal of yours, J-bird. But don't worry. With that right hook, we'll make a Morningstar of you yet."

The first day of lunch detention was super boring. Josephine spent it staring at the back of the desk in front of hers, wonder-ing whose floaty long hair had got caught between the rivets of the chair and the stone-blue back. Kayleigh Grace or the X-boys definitely would have mentioned if they just went around getting their hair caught in chairs all day. It seemed like the kind of thing people should warn you about.

The second day was better. Josephine ate the almond butter sandwich her mom had packed—enjoying the crunch of plain potato chips slipped between the almond butter and the jelly—and wondered what Cressida and Joshy were up to without her. She hoped Cressida wasn't mad anymore. Maybe she would message her during study hall when they were supposed to be reviewing quizzes on their Chromebooks.

Caught up in daydreaming after she walked out of the office, Josephine didn't notice the girl standing by her locker until she nearly bumped into her.

It was Riley Jane Mercer, dressed in dark blue cat ears, denim shorts, and a T-shirt to match. Her shimmery eye makeup made her look older and glowy, like a cool elf from one of Monty's favorite movies, and Mr. Cohen's bathroom pass was sticking out of her back pocket.

"Josephine, right?"

"Yeah." Josephine didn't know what to say. It was the first time a popular kid had spoken to her without seeming like they wanted to crush her under their shoe. "Um, hi."

Riley gave her a thin smile. "Hey. So, this is kind of weird, but I found this in some stuff yesterday. And I think you said you were looking for it?"

She produced a rolled-up piece of heavy paper. Josephine unrolled it and gasped. The fishbowl!

It didn't seem too messed up, either. One corner was dog-eared and kind of wrinkly, but no part of it was ripped or stained, and all the colors looked exactly like she'd remembered. She wanted to screech out loud but settled for pressing the top of the paper against her middle, almost hugging it.

"Where'd you find it?"

Riley shrugged. "Looked through my packet last night. Turns out it was stuck to the back of my watercolor. I guess because Miss Houston organizes stuff alphabetically."

Josephine didn't know what to say. "Probably."

"And it's really cool," Riley added. "I like the way you've shown all the light in this corner, by the hairclips."

Josephine had never heard another kid compliment her art before. Not to mention one of the most popular girls in their grade! It was like standing in the middle of the sun.

"Anyway." Riley motioned back toward the middle school hallway with a thumb. "I gotta go back to Pre-Algebra before Mr. Cohen goes insane."

"Wait!" Josephine rolled the fishbowl back up and set it carefully by her locker. So many words were trying to leap out of her throat, but the most important ones were for a certain best friend, who was also stuck in Pre-Algebra with insane Mr. Cohen. "Actually, can you take a note to someone else for me? If that's okay?"

Riley's face was open and friendly. "Sure."

FOUR WEEKS LATER

Basketballs thudded against the rubber gym floor, their rhythmic crashes echoing around and around the gym as the team got ready for warmups to start.

Josephine wasn't watching. She was lying on the middle step of the bleachers, reading a book of intertribal stories she'd had since fourth grade.

She'd just gotten to the part about a boy entering his first Junior Fancy Dance Powwow when she felt a tap on her shoe.

"Skibidi toilet!" Cressida's grinning face popped over the top of the pages.

"Shut up!" Josephine shoved Cressida away with a roll of her eyes before sitting up and marking her place in the book with a slip of paper. "You sound like my dumb brother."

"There're worse people to sound like," Cressida said airily, pretending to be kind of high and mighty with her nose pointed at the rafters. "Plus, Monty's kind of hot if you squint."

"Ew." Josephine shoved her again. Saying that was worse than a thousand skibidi toilets. "Just 'cause you think you'll get boobs soon does not mean my dumb brother is hot."

Cressida was still giggling as she shoved her hair back into place. "Well, I could be like Kristian and Maxim and talk your ear off about how amaaazing Wolverine is."

"God, please don't. I can't take any more superheroes. Joshy should never have introduced the X-boys to us."

"Speak of the devil," Cressida said, waving to someone behind her. Josephine turned and saw Joshy walking over with his own showcase drawing clutched in one hand: a self-portrait in bright pastels. "You finally taking that thing home?"

"Miss Houston wants me to enter it into the county fair next month," he explained as he walked over. "Said I should keep it somewhere safe until then."

He gave Josephine a look over the top of his glasses that she couldn't figure out. "Also said you're supposed to enter the fishbowl, and to make sure I reminded you."

Warm pride filled Josephine's chest, like water being poured into a glass pitcher. Miss Houston had asked her about it on Monday, before school, and Josephine had screeched so loud in response that she was sure she'd scared some birds out of bed. "My mom's signing my permission slip tonight."

"Good." Joshy bumped her arm with an elbow.

"Okay, shut up about art for a second," Cressida said, motioning them closer. "You know how Riley Jane and Brayden broke up again. For real this time?"

Everyone had heard that, Josephine didn't say. "Yeah, obviously."

Cressida put one hand next to her mouth to keep the entire gym from reading her lips. "So, Diana told me that Kayleigh Grace told her that Bella Beaulieu said it's because Riley has a crush on someone else. Maybe not even a *boy*."

"Uh-uh," Joshy shook his head. Now that they were real friends, they knew he was the authority on lots of gay things, since his sister Rhiannon always let him watch Drag Race on weeknights and he'd admitted to a big crush on that long-haired blonde guy from the vampire show. "She hasn't been single since fourth grade. I don't buy it."

"Well…." Josephine was remembering the pink thank-you note she'd put into Riley's locker, the day after Riley had given her back the fishbowl. And the sheet of fancy glitter stickers she'd found next to her seat in art, two days later. Name-brand, with Japanese writing on the back. Nothing like what Mom always bought at Walmart. "You never know, right? Maybe it's another mystery?"

Cressida's grin was sharper than a fresh pencil. "J-bird, I like the way you think."

Dear lil' rez girlies

Danielle Shandiin Emerson

Nizhoníyé—
> I see you, little rez girlies
> in the reflections of sunsets lining
> > łitsxo / sheen orange bluffs.
> With wet feet, easygoing hair—
> > > glittering
over lakes, specks of silver, found on roadside flea markets
and in
> > masaní's velvet wallet, where she
> > > keeps chuckling coins.
I see you
> eyeing that tiger's blood snow cone,
masaní sees it too.
She'll buy it and smile as you whisper
> a shy,
> dinilchíí' / pinked cheeked
> > > *Ahéhee' / thank you.*

Nizhoníyé—
> raise your hands little rez girlies
> and reach at juniper,   pull yourself into the cedar
> trees,   pick wild berries   your amá / mother
> used to say were poisonous,   just to keep
> > you and your cuzzins

from slipping them onto dry tongues,
        staining nail beds
lilac with ever-present sap, found on
                akézhoozh / toes
and agod / knees, then mistaken for bruises until
        the juice smeared
            off your fingers
        for days afterward,
           still easygoing.

Nizhoníyé—
    are the smiles that adorn little rez girl faces
    like   turquoise jewelry,
        the bits of sun loved cheeks
    made smooth,
      resembling
abalone shell and turned warm by amá's
    palms, pulling our chins up,

        up,
          up / deigo

          deigo

              deigo
when we speak Diné Bizaad, asking your
    cheii
from across an old creaking table,
to pass the   salt / Ashííhí shána'ááh.

& sharing your clans with Navajo strangers
        because kinship
            is lived together.
            Coating shí dóó shídiné'é futures
                in the old
                honey warm
                    beauty,
            the dried stems of Navajo tea, bundled in
            shimasaní's kitchen,
Nizhoníyé—she says, and our faces break into
            new dawn   smiles, traveling the path
                of the sun.

feasting rituals

jaye simpson

endear yourself to me
                on some off chance
that my lips
         should become a slanting prophecy
                   on the twisting spires
         of your own flesh, just above the beating muscle:
tantalizing rubied drink.

i stand at the entryway
         beckoning those curly brunette crowned lovers
               that may allow me this respite of consumption
         pulling my hips up   &   swallowing my swelling nipples
this entrancing frenzied feeding
         an utmost important undoing:
               i can return when we've had our fill.

like some slicing fruit,
               the peeling of thin skin, revealing those jeweled
         bite worthy morsels, feed me slice by slice
         with your own incisors.

didn't shauna love jackie so much
               &   don't you love me?
peel enough of my humanity back
                &   what a fine course i could make
         right before you: divine this fleshy buffet.

my gilded eyelids, fluttering cacophonous lashes,
        murder of crows as faithful daughters
    like the many winged tomorrows–
        i am dipped into as if i were some jar
    of fireweed honey or bear grease
        smeared upon lip
           or lapped up feverishly.

oh my sweet skinned mouth!
    ensure of me this feast before them! may they eat their fill!

The Oklahoma Ocean

Chelsea T. Hicks

May wears a fuchsia dress for Hailee's wedding. Hailee—who's marrying an unknown male. At least, unknown to May.

When they were younger, Hailee and May would wrestle each other on the floor to see who would have to get ready for cheerleading first. A nip on the nose signaled defeat. They felt better than the girls who sat on boys' laps behind the gym to smoke, but really, they didn't date because they had fathers who went into rages about small things, like misplaced shoes and plopping on the couch.

After high school, they went to different colleges. But Hailee dropped out to join the army, and now, there was this rogue marriage. May got on TikTok. There was nothing. No updated profile picture of Hailee since prom, when they went together as best friends. May didn't ever have a boyfriend in high school.

Over Christmas break, she'd visited her English teacher who told May that Hailee was dating. "I didn't think either of you was the type to just go get a boyfriend," said Mrs. White. "Do you have a boyfriend?"

May had shaken her head, embarrassed, the tops of her ears getting hot. She'd invented an excuse to leave.

When she got back to school, all her roommates had boyfriends, too. They'd all joined the Native sorority on campus, and they were rarely around.

As she gets ready for the wedding, May avoids putting on the dress. There is no one there to help her zip it up and she doesn't want to think about it, but the aloneness and the struggle of trying to zip the dress really stresses her out. She shouldn't have to be alone, no Hailee, no friends, no boyfriend, no help, no anyone.

After makeup, sparkle spritz body spray, brushed teeth, jewelry, shoes, hair pins—everything—May steps into the dress and really flings her right arm back over her head, holding the two panels of the dress together while she reaches for the zipper with her left hand. She grabs it and hikes it up until she is encased and thinks she should've joined the sorority. She tries to ignore that thought by checking her phone. As she scrolls on social media, in the background of her head she is regretting not only that she didn't rush for the sorority, but also her perpetual notions of superiority. She had told herself she wasn't the sorority *type*. She'd said sororities would be about too much partying, and she wanted to be a lawyer. But here she doesn't even have a best friend anymore.

The text from her ride pops up on her phone, and she jumps up, grabs her purse, and runs out of the house feeling afraid of life. Everyone else is living when she hasn't given herself permission to do anything except feel guilty.

"So, she's changing things up again," May says aloud as she runs down the dorm stairs, self-conscious that she's talking to herself. But hearing the noise outside her own head helps calm her nerves. She thinks of the save-the-date card on her bulletin board, pasted over her vision board filled with dark academia study memes. In a matte wedding mailer, Hailee stands in front of what appears to be an ocean, her right hand placed on the man's chest as if she learned womanhood from a vintage Sears catalogue found in a Goodwill.

What ocean is that? May wonders again.

Hailee is more the type to race around the pond on four wheelers, and to barrel race on a freshly broken mustang and compete about who can get into the higher-level math class. In May's sociology class she found out this is called androcentrism, meaning how it's considered cool for girls to act like boys, but taboo for boys to act like girls.

Her plus-one, Chris, isn't in that class with her but she always sees him right before it, during biology. He's sitting in his old Ford Bronco and she blushes because for some reason she remembers right then all the times he's seen her scrutinize the save-the-date in class. She was initially using it as a bookmark in the months leading up to the April wedding. Whenever her attention wondered from the lecture, Chris tilted his head to the side and looked at her with big eyes. It would make her laugh and they tried desperately not to make noise, she was imagined how he would think of her being all dressed up for this event she'd veritably been obsessing over for *months*.

He leans over and punches the door handle, pushing it open for her. "Hey," he says. He's wearing a surprisingly dapper close-cut suit that she has no idea where he got.

May giggles. "Hey." She grabs the handle on the ceiling and hoists herself up into the car. The suit, it makes him look very rich, which she's realizing he could be. Why did she assume he was like her?

"Ready to see your bestie pledge in sickness or health?" he says.

She smirks as she texts him the address, for some reason thinking of Hailee's brown hand covering the fiancé's heart in the save-the-date, as though pledging allegiance to him. For him? That would be more normal, considering Hailee is someone who loves America but in a complicated way.

"No, I'm not ready. I don't want to meet a ride or die I've never even met. But I've been thinking about it, and I wonder if it's kind of a military thing. Like, he's in the military. Hailee's grandfather fought in the military as a Native veteran. I guess he was a code talker for her tribe. I didn't even know there were code talks from all different tribes."

"A man who was proud to have earned his own citizenship, doubtless," said Chris.

The way the two of them are on the save-the-date, they don't look complicated. They look like normal American soldiers, a brown one and a white one, common as the days of the week.

The man's crinkled-up cheeks appear in her mind. There's something strange about the way the crinkles frame his smile, with an effect somewhat like a dimple but more masculine. A set of parentheses holding the sides of his mouth.

"Last time I talked to Hailee, she'd just got a military promotion, and she had a cheating a boyfriend, and he had a dishonorable discharge. It was dramatic. I feel like I don't know her. But I don't know *why*, you know?"

"Mm," Chris says, like he's savoring a good broth that's lingering in his mouth. It's sort of suggestive. She's driving but she glances over at him, annoyed. "Maybe she was waiting to break out and be someone new all along," he says.

May wants to ask *why would you say that?* But she just stares straight ahead at the flat roads of the city, judging herself again for not being the one brave enough to go and live.

"Did I tell you that she also got a demerit for signing up as white. Which, for some reason, *Chris*, she didn't tell them she was Native. And then the military comes across her blood quantum in some record, and she gets in trouble? I mean, what?"

"Mmhmm. Something obviously happened at some point," Chris says.

"All I can think when it comes to Hailee is *what*?" she concludes.

"Well, I'm curious, at this point. Especially after watching you with that little invite," he says. "What was Hailee like in high school?"

"Not flirtatious. Quiet. Mostly. There was this one time. Mainly I was the one to edge into maybe-popularity in middle school and high school, while Hailee criticized me. All 'you're better than them' type of comments."

"What was the one time?"

"Well. Our high school shut down and we had to switch schools. She left a semester earlier than me, like, her family predicting the school would close while mine waited 'til there was no other option. When I got to the new school, there was no more straightened hair and thick eyeliner and anorexia and silence. Now, she was curly-haired and curvy and laughing."

"Maybe she's figuring out who she is," said Chris.

"I guess," says May, and they turn on his mix CD—his condition for going to the wedding, he'd said. That he is the DJ. As Nirvana plays, May keeps thinking. She wonders if she and Hailee were protecting each other from men because they were jealous of the other one, but that can't be it. Can it? If it's not that, what is it? She cares a lot about what Hailee does, but Hailee seems to be breaking away, and it hurts.

She's glad she's brought Chris along, though. It makes her feel more secure to seem to have a possible boyfriend. When Hailee surveys the crowd at the wedding, she'll see this. And he's the person who has watched May stare and stare at the save-the-date every Monday, Wednesday, and Friday, so right now, he's the person who knows her best.

There's something else too, though. About Chris. It's like he's watching and waiting for something this mailer and this friend and this wedding is bringing out of her, and she feels seen. Whatever the exact reasons, she is glad.

"I like you," she says between songs. "You know, I always like to know the DJ."

"Whatever," he laughs. He smiles at her. "I'm happy to come."

Post indie comes on next. His taste is subtypes of indie music that May likes but usually avoids because she's trying to stay floating above the sadness, not aestheticize it. But she doesn't feel too sad. It actually feels appropriate as they roll through the multicolored grasses between Tulsa and Oklahoma City and it begins to rain.

She takes an exit for a spot where she likes to stop for coffee.

"You know that ocean-looking thing on the save-the-date for this wedding?" she says.

"That thing you stare at with the pasty guy on it," he says. "Yes. I know what it is,."

"You do?"

"Yeah. It's the Boone-Roubidoux Aquifer Sea."

"The what?" She remembers learning about aquifers when she was little, when fracking replaced the plugged oil wells. "I mean, I kind of remember aquifers being big, but I thought they were underground caves, not oceans?"

"Yeah, they are, like small little caves with water throughout them. Boone and Roubidoux aquifers collapsed into each other. The impact ended up sinking the surface ground above them down beneath the water. Because of all the fracking, they're totally salinated. It's undrinkable. The governor rebranded it as an ocean."

"How do you know this?" she said.

"The governor was my dad."

May pulls into the parking spot and turns off the engine. It takes her a minute to figure out what to say.

Chris stares at her, waiting for a reaction.

"So, your dad was the very last governor of Oklahoma?"

"The very last one before the tribes took governance of the state. Yeah. My dad hated that federal ruling."

May looks at Chris directly, unsure why he wouldn't have said anything. "You know I want to be a lawyer," she says.

"I know." He smiles. "May, my dad isn't a great guy. But that doesn't mean I can't be." He jumps out and jogs around the car and opens the door of the car for her and then strides into the coffee shop beside her like it was his idea to go here.

May stares at the back of his head as they get in line. She knows so little about this guy. All she really knows is that he drinks matcha lattes and plays phone chess during class.

Chris turns around to her and leans a little into her. "So, this ocean from the save-the-date, according to the wedding address in my phone, it's in Oklahoma. I think it really is the sea," he says. "Cause that's where we're headed. She's having the wedding at the *aquifer canyon.*"

Watching Chris talk, May is struck by what feels like his defining quality—she isn't sure of the right word to name it. Here-ness? He has good posture and friendly habits, like bringing coffee and cross-checking notes, always being on time. He's the kind of person you can take anywhere. He's just *there,* wherever he is. Maybe it's "self-assured," May thinks. Maybe it's "present."

"You're the son of a governor," she says out loud.

"Yep," he says, and turns to put in his order just as the barista is glaring at him. Outside, rain begins again. There is a wind rising, and signs creak on the storefronts at the edge of the new development, where gray clouds proliferate overhead.

"No coffee," May says to herself, processing that one of Oklahoma's famous out-of-nowhere storms is coming in, she chides herself she was so lost in her thoughts earlier she didn't even look outside. She says Chris's name, almost a whisper.

When Chris doesn't immediately turn back from the pick-up spot where he is waiting for his drink, she reaches for his hand.

"Hurry," she says. "We can't get stuck in this storm. I have a fear of thunder."

He follows her back to the car, leaving his coffee.

Severe weather change was, in the end, what gave control of the land back to the tribes. The environmental companies won enough cases at the federal level and so many died from tragedies that the tribes were able to sit between their treaty rights and their colonial power networks and their gaming compacts and their survival offerings. They got control of water via the courts and eventually became the dominant government. It didn't mean they weren't corrupt. May hadn't even known about the Boone Aquifer collapse, but her tribe had been involved in oil drilling.

Around that time, there were so many other disasters. Twisters, hurricanes, floods, and earthquakes in areas that had never had them before. It was like they went through everything at once.

As they speed out of the parking lot, the other patrons evacuate, following them, and they drive without any music on as shadows chase the land.

This is the beginning of a tornado. Dark clouds release torrents of rain, a huge wind rises, peeling off one of the signs of the coffee shop just as May and Chris get back on the interstate. They can hear the loud creaking. Because of the micro-climates, they don't know what the weather will be once they reach the wedding. It could be relatively sunny and clear. Everything depends on which way the wind is blowing.

Chris drives 110 mph in silence until they are in sunlight and then slows down and puts the music back on. A funnel reforms on the horizon in the distance of the rearview mirror, at the edge of OKC, where it will undoubtedly form a mess of shredded siding and unrooted trees.

"We have about forty minutes left," May finally says.

"Let's listen to music."

"OK," May giggles. She knows the first song, and they sing.

At a huge pile of corn husks, they go left and see the cut into the deep aquifer canyon. Chris puts his window down and dust rumbles up from the gravel road. They feel the wet air, and smell fresh coffee, and wood fire smoke.

"Is that Hailee?" says Chris.

It's Hailee in a clearing on a beach at the bottom of the sloped road, her form growing fully real as they near her amidst the trees that have grown in the collapsed earth at the edges of the aquifer sea. Hailee doesn't turn to them until they're right on her. She's standing over a boil pot on top a metal grate over a dwindling fire. Her yellow sundress has a bikini top underneath, peeking out the halter. It's flirty, tenth-grade Hailee, just the same way May never remembers her and still can't get used to.

May jumps out of the car. "Hey!" she says. "Happy wedding?

Suddenly she's aware of her outfit, how it doesn't match Hailee's.

Hailee, who is looking May up and down with discontent. The fuchsia dress, then over to Chris in the driver's seat. "What are you doing?" she says. It reminds May of the times she flirted with the white guy in debate class, who Hailee considered too arrogant. "Why are you here?" Hailee says, her voice rising. "Didn't you get my email?" She looks angry, and she's barely masking it with a fake upspeak.

May feels herself begin to be angry right back at Hailee, maybe permanently now. She's wondering if the only thing she and Hailee liked in each other was a brief childish possessiveness. Now that their personalities are chosen from the list of normal adult affect 1s, 2s and 3s, with subtype a, b, c, or something like that, May has failed to choose the most normal one, and so now they're doomed to hate each other. She doesn't know how to judge who the weak one is, and amidst all the accusations in her head, she really just feels that she's lost herself in losing her childhood best friend.

She begins to cry.

"Oh my god!" yells Hailee. "I have the canceled wedding and it's you who I have to comfort? Oh my god!"

Chris comes to stand beside May and pats her on the back.

Hailee sighs loudly and comes over to hug May. "You better not make me cry," Hailee says, her voice so low and quiet it's clear she wants to.

"So, you're not getting married?" says Chris, which makes May laugh.

"I'm sorry," May says. "I'm just so confused. You didn't even tell me you were getting engaged."

"You don't even check your email," said Hailee. "And no. I'm not getting married. And if I was, you'd be late."

"There was a tornado chasing us," offered Chris.

"Shouldn't that have made you more on time?"

"See?" said May. "She's aggressive. Not the sweet, flirty, marrying kind."

Hailee sinks onto a log then and puts her head in her hands. "I was here so I could reflect about that."

May and Chris look at each other, agreeing they should distract Hailee. Hailee's dusty Jeep is parked by the canyon wall. May remembers to announce Chris formally. "This is my plus-one, he's my study partner from bio. He's not such an asshole that he requires people to be sweet and flirty."

He walks over pulling on his lapels and extends his hand. "That's right." He smiles.

Hailee glares at him, then looks at May.

It feels like Chris is the person inferred between May and Hailee, the inversion of their tension, the one holding the jokes they will need. She wishes this is true and relaxes, and they sit down on the fallen trees arranged in a circle around the smoking fire and watch the embers.

May watches Hailee. The rising moon is at her earlobe, like an off-center earring. For a moment, all they hear is the wood popping, and the leaves of the trees shaking in the wind.

Hailee's stiff and strict posture loosens. "Do you all want to come back home with me?"

May and Chris trail Hailee back down her wedding dirt country road, back onto the county roads for about one mile, until they reach Hailee's large house. It is near the edge of the aquifer, somewhere in Shalagi Nation. It's baby blue and has a front porch with a swing, shutter windows, and a red door with a brass knocker.

"Military money," says May.

"She's a Captain?"

"I don't know her rank."

"Bad friend."

May doesn't like that, but she wonders if it's true. Maybe there's something about her that drove Hailee away. She isn't sure what she ever did to lose Hailee's trust, but she has a sense it's more who she *is*. So similar to Hailee, yet also not. White versus Native moms. The fact that Hailee's family had the money to go to a better school when May's didn't. There must be more, still. Their dads are both mean and what people call "abusive" or "strict," depending on your politics, something May's learned about in her first-year composition course. It's hard to keep track of where the resentment sprang up, but it's been there, May is now sure of that.

Hailee is ushering Chris inside first and walking them through an open floor plan that May's dad would call "urbane" even though they're in the middle of the countryside. May doesn't really understand how Hailee views this place. To her, it seems like a McMansion, but it's also so clean and Hailee seems to be proud of it. May is the pretentious one, and she feels bad. But she isn't sure whether to admire the commitment to bougie or be jealous and judgmental.

She watches Chris who is nodding and listening to Hailee explain the refrigerator's little shelves that pull out. She's looking lovingly at the marble countertops. Sinking into the large leather couch where she invites them to sit, across from a gas fireplace she turns on with a remote. May sits in a one-and-a-half chair beside the couch, across from a bookcase of fantasy and romance novels. Beyond that, the kitchen they've just toured, full of white ceramic this and that and a little generic farmhouse looking signs that say things varying slightly on "I'm home." May feels truly disappointed. She is too exhausted to think, but she feels. Her bones tell her that she was the one who worked on actual farms as a child. She would never pick a sign like that, romanticizing a farm and manual labor. She doesn't want to be different—less-resourced, as the school therapist says—but she tries to focus. She closes her eyes and imagines her and her roommates working together on everything, visiting with each other, so things aren't so hard.

She remains sitting there though as the other two start pouring drinks in the kitchen. They don't even care she's lost in her mind, and May tells herself to stand, but can't convince herself. On her phone, she searches "the ocean." There is a photo of a white girl underwater, taken from below as she swims to the surface on her board after wiping out. Foam grasps her body. Hailee is darker than that color, properly brown, whereas May is not. Yet, May has two Native parents—not one, like Hailee—so she's always been more involved in tribal stuff. This could be a reason to resent her. She has status, which according to sociology, is a way of hoarding resources. In this case, it's social validation and how that is connected to survival? Something like that. But maybe Hailee doesn't feel like she's found a place to belong, compared to May. The thought makes May feel guilty and she lays down and stares at the ceiling fan. It looks very expensive. May almost growls as she gets up and goes to the kitchen with hatred on her face.

Hailee is saying something about her Shalagi family and a boat. "My uncle left me a boat," she says. "It's not on an ocean, but it is a salt sea so big they call it *The Ocean*."

"We know about it." It's the aquifer, May realizes. "That's what was on the save-the-date."

Hailee continues talking, not even looking at May. "My uncle just gave me a slip of paper with an address written on it," Hailee goes on. "It was for a boat dock at that exposed aquifer harbor, the one that got bombed out the last time they tried the fracking on the Ocean, and then it got rebuilt and they stopped extracting."

"Can we ride the boat?" says Chris.

Hailee's voice gets intrigued by that, pausing, going up, but not in a fake way this time. "Are you guys staying?"

"We could," May says. She wants things to play out between them. She wants to dig into it.

"*The boat* is a long story. Even just to tell you about it. I'm not even talking about riding the boat, I'm just saying the boat's very *existence* is a whole thing."

May stares at the remote control for the fireplace. "I like stories more than weddings," she says.

This remark earns a second smile from Hailee, who seems pleased that May is acting hurt. "A *you* thing to say," she says.

Chris joins May in the living room and they sit.

"So you really don't want to hear the long story of why I'm not getting married today?" Hailee asks.

May really doesn't. "It's a fair trade," she says. "It seems painful and cruel to make you talk about that. Of course, we want to know." But she doesn't. And Hailee seems to want to talk about it. Why? Who is this girl? "We came here for your wedding," she continues, "But instead of dealing with that, I would be happy with the story of your boat." There is almost a growling quality to her voice, but Hailee seems giddy with it. It's as though she wants the tension to emerge, too. Chris is looking back and forth between the two of them like he's barely keeping up. May leans back in her seat and closes her eyes. "OK. Go."

"There she is," says Hailee. "There's my May. All strict."

May knows that when tragedy strikes, Hailee prefers distraction to grieving. This means she must not have really cared about this ex she wants to talk about. *That* means she must be in love with someone else. May just wants to know who, and quick. This could offer more clues as to why they've grown apart. Too many bad things happened, and Hailee didn't want to process it. She distracted herself with love the way May distracts herself with little chores and social media.

Between the wedding, and the boat, this story is also the Native one. May doesn't want to know about the white guy who jilted her, but her uncle from the Quah.

Despite her house and her pretensions, Hailee is still Native, May reminds herself.

Hailee smiles and toasts. "To the constantly unfolding story," she says.

They drink.

"Tell it like a book," May says.

"My friend dropped me off at the boat's address. My car was broken, and I was just out of basic. I wasn't talking to my parents, after my mom cheated."

"What…" May starts.

Hailee holds up a hand.

"This is not that. I'm not talking about dark family stuff right now, OK?"

May yields, both hands going up. "OK." She knows her friend. "The story at hand!"

Hailee begins. "So I got out and went into the place. It was the right address. It had to be. There was nothing for miles and miles. It was a two-story wooden house with stairs leading up to a small reception room with red velvet carpet and scratched faux wood walls. I rang the bell. It was kind of a shack, at a big parking lot full of old boats. I still don't know why. My friend already left, gone quick. He said he could only give me the ride here and he knew someone who could come pick me up if I couldn't get out of there. He said I'd have to let this guy know and he put the number for this friend on my phone. So, my friend was headed back to training camp, and it was just me and a short gray-haired man that came springing out of the back room. 'What can I do you for?' says the man."

"Wow," Chris said somberly. "That's dangerous. Something could've happened to you."

May almost grabs and squeezes Chris' hand but stops herself. Chris sees this and he turns and winks at her, which causes her to bounce in her seat. Live a little, she tells herself. She feels proud. Maybe Hailee is rubbing off on her. And maybe she's tired of being a coward. Hailee is shrugging, mentioning how it was a weird time and she didn't mind risking her safety.

"This was… when?" May says, refocusing. "How long ago?"

"It was in the fall," Hailee says, glaring. "It was another guy, before this *last* one. So I say to this guy at this shack boat junkyard place, 'I have a boat at this address from Robbie, my late uncle?' And I slid him the piece of paper that my uncle left me."

Hailee looks pretty, now that she's calming down. But May's starting to get interested in the story, how it's in the middle of nowhere, and why is it a boat?

"The man glanced at the paper containing the boat's details. I expected him to keep his head lowered and lift his eyes toward me—a sort of seedy judgmental glance—but he didn't. He said, 'She's over here.' Then, he opened the door I'd come in and tore down the steps. I had to run to follow him. I thought of what Michael used to say—that was my then-fiancé—'I like it when you text me. You're thinking of me.' Sorry… Michael doesn't need to be in this. That was my other ex.

"There were these small garages behind the big house reception thing area, and the other garages were lined up like stalls, and the boat was in the left-center one. It was a white boat with blue arrows. Looking at the boat made me nervous. I asked the old man if the boat had a name. When I did that, he spun, pointing his chin up high at me and cocking his head so I had some mild side-eye.

'No,' he said. 'But that can change. She's a beautiful boat but do you know how to drive her?'

'No,' I said.

'That's common,' he said, nodding his head. I really wanted to use some of my combat on him in that moment, the pig, but then he said something interesting. 'I'll send Avira over,' he said. Avira. Who is Avira? He left the garage and I stood there with the boat. It occurred to me that we were not near water, as far as I knew. I started to get confused, kind of scared, finally. I did not have a truck. I would not be able to haul this boat. I wondered why the boat was even here.'"

The gas fireplace is warming the room and Hailee is giving off a familiar smell, it's sort of like bread and vanilla, and May wants to put her head on her friend's shoulder and sleep. Hailee is saying how the man took her up to a room. May perked up, alarmed.

"What?"

"Yeah! He was saying, 'Every garage storage and maintenance spot comes with a small room, you know, to leave teens in to watch TV while you're out or to change into boat clothes.' I thought that was weird, and I don't even think it's true, but I followed him up to the room, which was probably stupid, but like I said, I just couldn't manage to care much about anything at the time. It's like all my emotions were gone, almost my whole being. So I just went to the room. It was identical to the reception room, just to the left and down a few doors, like a motel. There was one window and once he had left me there with the key, I let all my breath out, thought it was good I wasn't dead, and stood and watched the long-bladed bushes shake in the light wind. There was a constant little wind. But then I remembered that there was someone named Avira."

"Avira," said Chris, questioningly.

May looked at him, part of her like *what are you doing* but part of her wanting him to push and pull and dig into the story.

She turned quickly back to Hailee, who was staring at the fire, rapt.

"I could see this Avira like a stone's throw away. She was standing facing away from me, long black hair cut straight, all of it on her back. I had once cut a boyfriend's hair in high school and knew that when you cut it straight all hanging down the back, it looks shorter in the front. Avira turned. Her hair did look like that, gradually shorter in the front. She had wide cheekbones, light skin, and almond-shaped eyes. She was short and wore a jean jacket tied on her hips. She was very beautiful."

"You never dated anyone in high school!" May interrupts.

But Hailee just looks at her, her full lips slack. "You always thought you were the popular one," she says. "But I had my time when I was away from you."

May's jaw drops and Chris squeals, as though imitating girls at a sleepover. "Oo!" he says. "You guys are kinda gay, huh? Have you two slept together?" He seems genuinely curious, and May looks at Hailee, her jaw dropping further. Hailee smiles hugely and pops her head to the side, flirting now, making her curls bounce around her head kind of like a Mustang. "I am not gay!" she enthuses. It comes off weird, like maybe sarcastic? It is so cringe that May realizes she, at least, might be gay.

"What's wrong with being gay?" May says.

"Ugh!" Hailee says. "Can I please keep on with the story?" Hailee gives Chris an evil look and it occurs to May that he might be here because he hoped they were gay, and this excited him. She can feel it in her bones, that he is trying to flirt with both of them now, and it doesn't make her angry, but she isn't sure why. She wonders if this has to do with her "ancestral" past here on this land or if she is gay or *what*. She is confused, but it makes her giddy. Forget her, she thinks, about Hailee, and the old sense of competition moves in. May just knows Hailee is going to get flirty now to protest this new accusation, so she readies herself and moves over into the one-and-a-half chair beside Hailee, putting an arm around her.

"Calm down, buddy," says May.

Hailee settles into her arm like she approves and goes on. "Avira said to 'follow me,' so for the next two hours, I did. We did all the chores necessary to keep a boat nice, none of which I knew about. It resembles the amount of work needed to load a horse into a trailer. But Avira also had a red truck, and she pulled it around and we hooked the boat up. We put WD-40 on its trailer wheels, which was the last step and finally, we got in and continued further down the same gravel road I had walked to get here. It was dark, and we eventually came to a cave with sand.

"'We have to push the boat through here,' Avira said.

"We unhooked it and pushed it. It seemed like it took a long time. Eventually we came to the water and pushed the boat off the trailer into the water. Then we hopped onto it and Avira turned the motor on and we rode over some low waves around a rock jetty and turned into a bright place with light blue water.

'This is *The Sea*," Avira said.

'Right. Oceans surround continents. Continents contain seas,' I said.

'Exactly,' said Avira. She liked me."

"Ooh, that's kind of sexy," says Chris.

"Oh my god!" May yells.

But Hailee is just looking at Chris steadily, her eyebrows flat and her brow sunk. "Are you gay?"

Chris smiles with his mouth closed, a look that May finds impossible to interpret. Her head is starting to get totally saturated, and she feels like she is going to scream. "I think I'm overwhelmed," she says. "I can't think."

Hailee grabs her hand, squeezes it, and keeps talking.

"'The rain filled the dust bowl. Before that, eons and eons ago, this was an ocean and that's what's with all the fossils. Now, we have a sea again,' that's what Avira said."

May interrupts again. "Wait? Is this real? I mean, I know about the fracking and stuff but is this a real story?"

Hailee makes a face at May. "You really are losing it." She leans her head forward and intones—her long, curly black hair shaking and her black eyes and small brown arms flashing in the firelight—"And I said to Avira, 'I'm afraid to drive a boat on my own!"

"Don't be," Avira said, but May is tuning out. She is thinking about all this gayness, what does it mean? Her mom had always said that it's not a sin to be gay, it's a sin to *live* gay or act gay. Like, this means that everyone is gay? So, if Hailee and May and Chris, for that matter, are not living gay with gay relationships, then they are not and can't be gay, at least according to this way her mom tells it? She feels like she's actually going to faint. Chris notices this and puts a hand at her back between her shoulder blades. She realized how uncomfortable the dress is.

"Can you unzip this?" she says. "I'm not trying to be weird. It's like, hurting me."

Hailee gets up and says she'll get a T-shirt and while she does May is just kind of dizzy and she's looking at Chris and they just lean in and kiss each other. His mouth is a little salty, and the taste of him makes her salivate. As soon as she realizes what she's doing she freaks out and jumps up as Hailee comes back in the room. May stops with the T-shirt at the threshold and Chris laughs smugly, with his mouth closed, his eyes crinkling in a smile that reminds her of the ex. May slowly sinks back down onto the couch.

"Since you asked," says Chris, addressing Hailee, "I'm bi."

"Your mom," says May weakly, thinking of her own mom and how he's *not* gay at the moment because he just kissed her, a born female involved in proscribed gender. She begins to laugh, and the way Hailee and Chris look at her, Chris sympathetically and warmly, and Hailee with judgmental confusion but also a hint of dearness, makes them all laugh. She takes the T-shirt from

Hailee and puts it on top of the dress and pulls the unzipped top half of the dress down around her hips.

"OK. Intermission over. Get back to it!" she yells.

"Where was I?" Hailee says, looking genuinely happy for the first time tonight. So, apparently, what she wants is freedom, May concludes. Chris is jogging Hailee's memory, and they are now driving the boat through the ocean with Avira.

"We went really fast and we took it back before the tide was too high. Avira said that the cove there was eastward facing so it had few waves, but we still had come up too close to the cave and the boat could wreck! She took it back out and then brought it in herself, driving the boat like a pro. It was almost storming. I wanted to invite her to do yoga videos with me in my room and eat some chocolate, but I thought it would be rude in case she didn't want to.

'How old are you?' she asked me. I didn't tell her but said it was rude, so she would know I was older than her, but not *how old*. She said she was sixteen. All this time I had been thinking she was about twenty. I went up to my room and napped. When I woke, it was too late to see what Avira was doing so I slept more on the carpet in my little red room and then around 3 a.m. I went to the beach."

Chris says, "Sorry, what were you doing, generally, in your life, at the time?"

"Furlough. Five months ago. Before Jim."

Chris shakes his head, meaning that she doesn't have to explain but he doesn't understand.

"I had nothing better to do. Like I told you, I could barely care."

"Got it…" says Chris. "I've never really been there, but I kind of feel like I'm there now."

May cannot believe these two. She wants to kiss Chris again. She feels like she's lost her mind. She tries to listen to the story to ground down to something calming.

"As soon as I got to the shore by the light of the moon, I cried on my boat because I knew that my ex—my ex of that time, not Jim—was probably drinking alone in his room and I was worried about him. I loved him. I couldn't really remember what had happened, like, really. I knew what it was, but I couldn't really believe it. Why, I kept thinking, weren't we together? I mean, he had cheated on me and also told me to abort our baby when I got pregnant, but I still didn't understand *why*. Yeah. He had cheated on me. I didn't know *why*, not really."

May started to cry because that was exactly how she felt with Hailee.

Hailee saw it but didn't stop talking, just wiped the lone tear, which made May feel a little better, and kept talking. "But I went out to the boat and I did yoga alone and I loved it. Things were uncertain on a minute-by-minute basis but I was fine. I wanted to name it, but couldn't think of what to call it."

"Wait," Chris says. "Is this ex the same one you were marrying?"

"I *was* going to marry that guy, my ex at that time, but it didn't get as far as the almost marrying of today, if that's what you're asking."

"Oh," May says.

"Ha!" says Chris.

"What did you end on, for naming the boat?" May asks.

"In the end, I chose 'Safe Haven,'" Hailee answers.

May was starting to kind of fall asleep, while also feeling turned on, and her blood moving just all around her body, but she listened to Hailee's voice say how she got seasick and how the sky was the same color as the water and it was all dark and the boat was moving so much that she was scared she'd get thrown off and how she tied a rope from her waist to the metal bars on the boat and gripped the steering wheel and tried to look out for rocks.

"That I would not crash into rocks. That was all that mattered. This continued for a long time until my skin hurt and my bones. But then the storm stopped, and there was a clear moon directly in the middle of the sky. I stayed up watching the moon. There was no land in sight."

"So, you were lost, your first time alone at sea?" Chris asks. "Do you know how to fish?"

That made May wake up a little bit, because it sounded like flirting, and it made her mad. She was really realizing how possessive she was. She took both of their hands and squeezed them.

"My grandpa taught me, yeah," said Hailee with a little devil grin that made May squeeze a little harder. "The fish bit quick and so I caught four and then cooked them on a little camping gas burner thing in the keep below that Avira had showed me. I figured it was time to go back so I went the direction of the sun since it was the same spot it had been where Avira and I went out before. Sure enough, I came to the cave and docked the boat and walked back. There were twenty-six missed calls on my phone, from Avira. I looked up and thought I saw three moons. But there were no missed calls from May."

May stops her. "Wait! Avira had called you twenty-six times? I'm sorry!" She felt herself turning bright pink on her face, neck, and chest. She wanted to say that Hailee had not been picking up the phone for months, so why should she expect her to care, but it was obvious that this was a time in Hailee's life when she would have needed anyone, and no one was there. To keep from drawing the attention, she forced herself not to cry this time. She knew why she was so emotional. It was from refusing to admit she was thinking all those thoughts about being superior and not having a boyfriend and not having friends and being lonely. She watched Hailee's face as Hailee cried this time.

"I'm sorry I never called you back that summer. I just thought you would judge me."

"I'm sorry," whispered May. "I'm sorry."

It was difficult to breathe, but she managed it and watched

Hailee so that Hailee knew to just keep going, that it was all OK.

But Hailee kept talking about them. "I just couldn't call with nothing but tragedy to say. You know how I hate talking about bad things. But when I got back to the shack boat junkyard place, and my room there, my old ex was waiting for me, and that was why Avira had called!"

"What!" Chris gasped.

"What…" May echoed.

"Uh, yeah. He had come and left. Both of them thinking I had died! And that was one of the times the emergency response was 'limited,' you know how it goes. So I just shook my head, I really couldn't believe it, and I went to my red-carpet room. That's what we called it. The venetian blinds were open, and it was cloudy. There was a little coffee maker on the one table in the room and a note. 'We have a Walmart cot here,' it said. I wanted to call my ex, but I was used to this desire and shrugged it off by reminding myself that he had wanted to abort the baby without really caring what I wanted, was committed to being a cheater, and he never called back. So I got a metal bowl from outside where rainwater had collected, just in this little bowl there, I don't know who put it there, and I washed my face. Then I brushed my teeth with the mini toothpaste and my hair with a brush in my backpack. I missed cooking. I used to cook tomato, garlic and eggs and dip toast in it for breakfast. I felt angry and frantic. That was probably my lowest point. I don't know why, but I felt like I was going to die. I wanted to feel the sensation of constant motion in my life. I wanted sun. I wanted the calm morning and leaves and a quiet, dark apartment where I could think, but I had nothing. No, that wasn't true. I had a room. In fact, I had a whole house I had left to visit this boat. I turned and ran to my boat. I tried to mentally shake myself into sense. On my run to the boat, I ran into Avira. I wasn't looking, and she wasn't either, and we somehow slammed full frontal in the chest. It really hurt."

"Oh!" said Chris.

"She was so happy to see me, though. I think it was then that she called my ex, after that."

"What!" said May.

"Well, she'd thought I'd died. She was emotional."

"Anyway. So I went on past Avira and took out my worry dolls. I have a Shalagi Grandma. The other one is mixed. She had given them to me and said to tell the dolls my worries. They were, like, these tiny wire people with cardboard heads and marked dot eyes, and they were clothed in wrapped string. So, I told them my worries. They looked like such respectable people, people ready to take on the worries of another because they had too few of their own."

"So, you're…" Chris clarifies.

"I said my Grandma is Creole. I mean, she was pretty passionate about saying she was white, but she wasn't. But she could pass, and that made my mom actually really white, I think, I'm not too sure how that works. If you can really get away from what your parents are, or not. But she never had any connection to anything. Anyway, I identify as German but back to the story.

"I was just so afraid that no one would ever want me. I was afraid I would never be able to rescue myself. But something had happened on the boat and in the night. When I returned to my room the second time, I found my ex-boyfriend there. Like I said, Avira must have told him I was alive. He had come back there. He was sleeping. I began to cry when I saw him and my stuttered breaths woke him only partly. I lay on my back beside him where he lay on his stomach. My relaxed patella looked so similar to the curve of his upturned heel that I almost thought they were the same. I was really tired. Eventually I fell asleep. We woke at noon. He said he wanted to take me to a coffee shop.

"'Why?' I said. 'You don't drink coffee.'

"He said, 'I know, but it's something I always meant to do.'

"Things had not ended well between us. It had been a month

since we'd spoken. So now he was here and taking me in his old battered up black truck to the coffee shop in the town nearby. I found out later he knew where I was because of my friend, and he had come to my house, where she was house-sitting. But I didn't think to ask him then."

"Wait," says May "So how were you feeling about all this? About him being there?"

"Well, I felt like it was a caring gesture to get me coffee, and he was attempting to give me closure, or else he was going to reconfess his love and say he would be faithful for me, but I knew that since he was taking me to a coffee shop it was at least an attempt at a kind act."

"Wow," says Chris. He put his hands in his lap. "What did your ex-boyfriend order?"

"He ordered hot chocolate. It was a small, spare place in dark wood, and empty except for a rack of magazines. We sat on the back deck in the sun, listening to the same music shared through headphones. It was very quiet and there was dappled sunlight filtering through the leaves of trees and the sun umbrella. It was nice. It turned out he said nothing at all. But on the drive back, he did. He put his hand on my knee and said, 'Hailee, I love you. I care about you.'

"Wait," says Chris. "What did you order, at the coffee shop?"

May cocked her head at him. "What? Why?"

He turns to Hailee. "I want the details."

Hailee looks between May and Chris, but May laughs. "Tell!"

"An iced Americano."

Chris smiles. "OK. Huh. What else did Boyfriend say?"

"Ex-boyfriend said, with his hand cupping my knee, 'Is it OK if I touch your leg?' And he went on squeezing my leg though I said nothing. He said, 'It's not fair for you to cut me off like this. I want to know how your career is going. I love you. I just… I would be monogamous for you, but I don't want to do that. I don't like it, I really don't. You're just so independent,' he said. That's what he said. *Independent.* I got the nerve to move his hand off my knee and said, 'That's fine, Michael.' Then he said, 'Come with me. You don't wanna stay here. We can go out, have some fun, and I'll fuck you like you like.' I wanted to laugh in his face, because he didn't have a clue. I just smiled and said I was busy, and I appreciated his visit, and that he'd been very nice to me. I said all that just so he would go away without a fight. He just wanted to have sex, anyway, and I thought it was a little funny he came all the way just for that."

"I don't think that was it," says May. I could tell he probably loved her, but he was just soft and emotional, like me, and probably distracted and selfish too, also like me.

Hailee smiled at me indulgently like she could read my mind. "Think whatever you want. I'm pretty sure he was a playboy."

"I'm a playboy," I said.

"You are not," said Hailee.

"She may be. May be," said Chris.

We all laughed, and it was sort of hard for May to stop. That made her cry, too, but she was starting to feel better. Not so tired, so delirious, so crazy, or so angry, or lonely. She felt good.

Chris looks at his hands folded in his lap. "I don't know. Keep going. Story's almost over."

She makes the expression from when she first conjured the story. "When my ex was gone in his truck, Avira asked me to get coffee. I told her I'd just had coffee, but we could eat snacks if she had them, in my room. I was hungry. 'I only have a carpet,' I stated. 'Fine,' Avira said. Avira came into my room and we sat on the carpet. She put a pile of candy on the floor, opened Twizzlers, parting the plastic in a long sinuous line with the delicacy of a person cutting pasta. I sort of felt in love with her. You won't believe this next part. I sat beside her and we kissed."

"Oh. My. God." May takes a huge breath. She looks at Chris, who is leaning forward, his palms cupping the tops of his knees, his lips parted in amazement. His eyes meet May's and they widen a little. Hailee is just gazing at the floor with a nostalgic half-smile on her face. May wonders if Hailee had ever thought of kissing her, or if May had been the only one that truly adored and deep down, had a thing for Hailee, source or origin unknown, but fact being.

"Something broke in me, again," Hailee said, softly sighing. "Since the last emotional outburst on the boat, I had not really talked to anyone. Of course, not Michael. I think that was why I took a risk like that, because of my loneliness. But then I remembered she was sixteen.

'I'm really sorry,' I said. Avira waved her hands and laughed.

'It's just a kiss,' Avira said, like I was lame. But I knew I could've gotten in trouble for that. At the same time, in a place like that, it seemed anything could happen and no one would know. That made me uneasy. I wanted to get out of there. So I did. I just left. I got the ride with my ex and he gave it to me, although he was kind of pissed off, we didn't sleep together, I think. That's how we ended it, with a game of bus driver. And I left the boat there too. It's still there."

May pictured Avira as a mixed girl with some junior mints and Twizzlers, playing with her food, leaning back on one elbow on the red carpet. She would be one to stay for a while and watch a movie on her phone.

Hailee gets up immediately after the story, going to her vintage DVD player and putting on *The Hobbit* without asking. May feels sad, but she doesn't say anything to either of them. None of them do. She falls asleep midway through, then Chris, and then Hailee.

They sleep until eleven, and May has the feeling that there is nothing more Native than staying up all night accidentally crashing out watching movies. In the morning, Hailee is making pancakes and telling Chris stories about army parties.

She finally has her leaves through the window, she has her house back, and May realizes this is all she needs.

"I miss you," May says. It just slips out.

"I'm coming back to school," says Hailee. "Dunno if you knew. Maybe we can live together, if you don't already have too many friends?"

"I didn't, I don't" says May, wiping away the sleep in her eyes, still stuck in the dream of this whole weekend. She could ask about her plans, but decides to go slow. "I know I have to go back to 'real life' or whatever. But do you guys still want to go to the ocean?"

They all look at each other, but no one needs to say a thing.

April showers.

Danielle Shandiin Emerson

picking the stems of ch'ilgohwehih

Shiyazhí, / my little one,   what will   you keep?
in the timber regions.   July heat,   Ya'iishjááshtsoh, orange bulbs
heavy-lidded, pressing my palms inwards.   Against my eyes.
Goat heads stack my spine, tethering my body
to desert sagebrush. My forearms
lock like dry weeds,   bunches of jade and olive
*   surrounding the irrigation ditch.*
Wax string wrapped around bundles of ch'ilgohwehih / Navajo Tea,
*   collected in white plastic Walmart bags from*
*   shimasaní's wooden cabinet.*
behind the rot eaten pantry door.
*   Hanging like ghost bead bracelets,*
they raise arms to ward off bad dreams,
*   along my cousin's*
*   wrist.*
*   Plucked from the side of the   old highway,*
where accidents seem predetermined, colliding like smeared
cicadas
*   on stovetop pavement.*
*   Shí éí unsure, / wholá,*

turning over dry dirt in shí hands, digging with oak twigs, as Navajo Tea

grazes my knees, and I step closer to the sky,

> *yágó dootł'izh, a baby blue jean jacket, where specks of*

shandiin / sunshine   fall like abíní / morning dew on

> *dew-loving skin.*

My cousin walks with her back tall, strong like ch'ilgohwehih

bluffs.

I want to cry, collapse my right thumb inwards, until my skin

is inside out.

> *But shiyazh, she says, watch the stars climb again,*

night

after night. They look like your sibling's eyes,

> *pools of fire stoked light.*

> *When people ask, what will you keep?*

Wrapped ch'ilgohwehih on my hands—

> *staining my fingers husk green.*

> *I'll keep their love,*

> *my cousin's strength, stems of Navajo brilliance refusing*

to bend

> *as cars drive by disturbing a budding nizhoní-ful*

> *silence.*

A fuss over mush

Amber McCrary

Soften your face like mush

Be like mush,
Think like mush!

Surrender! Soften the body!
No! Don't make your body too soft
It has to be slender like steel

That rock of a neck of yours
Must feel like masa—
nice steamed, fresh masa!
Can you smell it? Be a fresh girl!

No one wants a crusty kernel

Your skin is the husk
Let me devour it!

Don't think too much
Tension is not sexy
Think less
Don't think at all

If you can make it from point A to point B
Voila!
You found the secret to life!
Live without thinking!

Never mind your surroundings
People are trying to make it out just like you
People want to be mush
Why must we unravel our husks
for hard eyes
to throw to the crows

I unravel my husks
for discussions of everything
because I'm in love with everything

My rock of neck
 rests
on a cloud of pillows every moonlight

My body tenses each hour the sun laughs
but I'm grateful
because I can be

I surrender my teal masa of a mush
to my fingers

Punch each plastic word down
Light my screen up

Take up all the space I want
in pages
unlike in grocery stores
where I have to wait behind
the white guy
in front of the entire shelf of soup
for five minutes

His time and space can be all up anywhere
at anytime

with no consequences
critiques
or correctness

So once again, sweet girl
Soften your face
Don't think too much
Be like mush
if you wish for them to unravel your husks
and devour you

Amphibians made of Apple

Amelia Vigil

Amphibians made of Apple
a dell of dense fog
roofs muffin top upon the steel
birds lacerate the streets above
at one seventy-two, children stack like flapjacks
their sleep a bitter coffee, grinds inside
down the street the bushes float away
leaving pits flamingo leg deep
up the hill lizards lust in mailboxes
tails drip from slats made of beeswax
the bus driver signals left with her eyebrow
inhales smoke instead of bus fair
snorts at every red light
houses turn face to greet each other
wide panes smile with secrets
a murmuration of memory above slanting cement
yesterday a kickball lodged in the sun
and became the moon
the Redred orb
rainbowed above our house
taunting the children inside to come out
and the frogs
I forgot to mention the frogs

Sky Woman Rising: A Memoir

Moniquill Blackgoose

The old woman sat on a reedwork chair in the shade of a chestnut tree, a wooden cup cradled between her hands. Something like two dozen children were gathered on the ground at her feet, little ones sitting on older siblings' laps. Some were dressed in dancing finery, some in historical clothing, others in their day-to-day attire. Most had long hair, some dyed in vibrant colors. She knew each of the children, and their parents, and their grandparents. Many of them had heard this story before, in previous Founders' Day observances, but they'd all chosen to come and listen to her here and now. Sometimes it helped to hear a story more than once.

"Some of you know me as Mama Moth, and some of you know me as Okummus, and some of you might know me as 'The Dirt Lady' too. My *name* is Evelyn Papohkumis Greene, and this is my story," she began. The children paid close attention to her words. She was one of the eldest elders, after all, one of the last living founders.

"I was born in the year 2020 by the Gregorian calendar, which was the one commonly used at the location and time of my birth. I was born on earth, in a place then called Fall River. It was before the rematriation of Massachusetts. The earth's gone around the sun one hundred times and more since then."

She paused, taking a long breath, gazing at something in the distance for a moment. The sounds of other Founders' Day observances filtered through the trees, song and laughter. Moth preferred to be honored quietly these days.

She continued, "When I was a little girl, the earth was sick with a fever. She'd been fighting an infection called 'capitalism' from about the sixteenth century, and by the twenty-first century it was *bad*. Humankind didn't know, then, whether or not earth was going to get better. Governments moved with ponderous indifference, unable or unwilling to untangle themselves from fossil fuels. Islands sank, deserts grew, hurricanes pummeled coastlines. It was a very hard time for Earth, and for all the beings living on her—the family lines of many beings were lost to extinction. There were efforts to escape—expeditions launched by powerful corporations, who thought that space colonization was their manifest destiny. Sleeper ships and generational ones aimed at impossibly distant exoplanets. Underground colonies on Nanapaushat—moon—and on Noh Nanwusshau—mars. There were attempts at terraforming, at hydroponic farming in sterile bunkers lit with LEDs. It was prison labor they sent first, then the indentured. There were a million people on Noh Nanwusshau by 2050, all of them with a lifetime of debt to pay back to the company that had sent them there. People living like termites in concrete boxes deep underground, breathing recycled air, working long hours at soul-crushing work, mining and construction and fabrication. People whose souls were owned by the company store, who died by the thousands from the kind of sickness and injury inevitable under those conditions—breathing plastic fumes and microparticles day in and day out, eating food that had never seen sunlight. People not getting enough sleep, enough beauty, enough love. People whose bodies withered in low gravity, like seedlings grown leggy and pale under poor light. There were always more desperate people ready to replace the ones that did not survive. By the time the rich arrived at any of those colonies, an army of service workers was there to attend them. There was a vast migration of people with power and means, promised luxury living among the stars. People deciding to live in tin cans with fiddly mechanical life support systems. The best laid plans of people who believed that human beings were somehow different from all the rest of the beings on earth—better, more important. It ended poorly for every one of those colonies."

Moth paused again, taking a sip from her cup. She looked away into the middle distance, silent and reflecting for a moment. None of the gathered children interrupted or needled at her; this was how stories were told sometimes.

"I want you all to understand, my darlings, that no outsider has ever cared about the first people of the dawn lands—the part of Earth commonly known as New England. Our people were presumed extinct even before there was a nation called the United States of America, wiped out in the Pequod War and Metacomet's War, the survivors sold into slavery and scattered to the wind. The first apocalypse happened shortly before the year of their lord 1620—plagues of leptospirosis and smallpox were introduced from an alien world an ocean away, killing two thirds of our people before any white man ever set foot on our shores. One of my ancestors—one I share with a lot of you—was the great sachem Ousamequin. He treated with William Bradford, John Carver, and Myles Standish. It turned out poorly."

She took another sip of tea, looking pensive. Her gaze swept across the children, assessing their ages, their readiness to know certain things. The youngest of them were five or six, the oldest twelve or thirteen, on the cusp of adolescence. She made a deliberation and, nodding to herself, continued on.

"You probably know from school, some of you, that the Bureau of Indian Affairs was founded in 1824. The Indian Reorganization Act happened in 1934, the American Indian Religious Freedom Act in 1978, lots of other things like that. Agencies and authorities of the colonial government, Men of The United States—but they made their declarations and fought their wars with nations west of us. They thought that we were dead, buried, a problem already solved. The Narragansett only gained recognition by the colonizers' government in 1983. The

Aquinnah Wampanoag didn't gain recognition until 1987, and the Mashpee in 2007. Most of the survivors of those sixteenth and seventeenth century genocides, and their descendants, never gained recognition at all. Lots of different people spoke of us only in the past tense, insisted to us *'You are dead, you are gone.'* By the time I was born, we were used to being dismissed. The blood quantum purges and disenrollment declarations of the 2030s and 2040s weren't new to us. It wasn't the first time we'd been told *'You do not meet the definition of Indian.'* We survived, regardless."

Moth lifted her cup to her lips and tilted her head back, emptying the last of it, setting the cup down carefully on the ground near the foot of her chair. She smiled, but it was a painful sort of smile.

"It wasn't until the 2050s—after the collapse, after the war— that the Dawnland Confederation came together. The Mashantucket and the Mohegan in Connecticut. The Aquinnah and the Mashpee in Massachusetts. The Narragansetts and the Seaconke in Rhode Island. The Maliseet, Passamaquoddy, and Penobscot in Maine. The people of many small and landless nations, the people whose homes were washed away by rising seas and fierce storms as the earth's fever grew worse and worse. We were finally able to put aside petty enmities in the face of destruction."

Moth took a breath, frowning, considering.

"You kids all know the story of Sky Woman, yeah?" she asked. Enough little heads quietly nodded that she felt there was a consensus.

"There was once an island in the sky, and sky people lived there. When Sky Woman uprooted a tree, it created a hole in the world—one that she fell through to come to Earth. It's important to remember that to uproot a tree is to create a wound. The Dawnland Confederation kept that in mind, when building New Sky World. So many of the other projects, the ones that intended to leave Earth behind, didn't hesitate for a moment to extract materials from Earth to build their ships. They didn't ask, they didn't thank, they didn't return what they'd taken. In English—which I grew up speaking, because it was the dominant language at that place and time—there is no concept of animacy. No distinction between beings and objects; it doesn't recognize most beings as beings at all. That might be part of why so many of those projects failed—they were made without love, from stolen materials. The persons who made them were forced into it, their hands and hearts unwilling. Those colonies were made without *ceremony*."

Beyond the tree line, the song came to an end and there was stillness for a few moments. Nothing but wind in the leaves, and birdsong. The singers began a new song, and Moth continued her story.

"We knew, before we ever began to build New Sky World, that it was not an effort to leave the Earth. We always meant to stay beside her, as close as Nanapaushat, to carry some of her burdens while she recovered from her sickness. We built New Sky World's bones from stardust and mined asteroids because we knew that taking so much metal and stone away from the earth would wound her. We gathered water from comets and such for the same reason. By then, others on Earth had taken notice of what we were doing. Some of them tried to copy our methods, but without understanding the ceremony of it. They saw and agreed that an ecosystem could only maintain itself as a whole but weren't patient enough to build one. They scooped out pieces of ecosystems and housed them on orbital stations, like uprooting a tree from the forest and trying to replant it in a park. They were surprised and angry when the trees they'd uprooted died."

Moth paused again, and in the companionable silence one of the children raised a hand. Moth acknowledged them with a nod, and the child asked,

"There are other places than New Sky World though? I've got 'net friends from Vittana Nagaraṁ, and Jojolo, and Taonga, and Hadiqat Fi Alsama'?"

"That's true," Moth said, nodding. "There are other places; other people and cultures and philosophies that were able to understand the needfulness of ceremony, of preservation of *place* and the relationship of people to it when building new worlds. There were many successes, as well as many failures. Our world, New Sky World, carries a very specific biome—we're a northeastern woodland of the kind found on Turtle Island. Other worlds carry different biomes, different creatures with different ways of being. Can any of you tell me what the rarest and most precious substance on Earth is? The thing that all life needs?"

A child, eight or nine years old maybe, raised a timid hand. Moth nodded. "Wuskáukamuck," the child said. Soil

"Exactly," Moth said with a warm smile. "When Sky Woman first stood upon Turtle's back, the thing she most needed was soil. She couldn't get it alone; she had to ask for help. Muskrat brought her mud from the dark depths beneath the waters and gave his life in the effort. Sky woman gave her thanks, and Turtle Island was made from gifts and gratitude. It is only by gifts and gratitude that any world can be born and thrive. I made it my life's work to know soil, even before our people had imagined New Sky World. I studied plant and soil sciences at UMass, and the knowledge I gained there was one of the reasons that I became a founder of New Sky World. The substance of Nanapaushat and Noh Nanwusshau, of all the asteroids and star bodies, is not soil. There's no word for that substance in our tongue, but in English it's called 'regolith'. There is no life in it, and so it cannot support much life at all. We who made it our work to build soil for New Sky World sought out the fiercest and most determined of beings to help us, asked them to be a part of what we were building. We asked the smallest of beings—bacteria. We asked the eldest of plants—algae, moss, liverwort. We asked our relations neither plant nor animal—fungi. We introduced them to regolith, and offered plenty of water and sunlight, and asked for their unique expertise. We gathered food for them from Earth, mindful to take only what could be replenished—mostly the bodies of trees that had already been killed by Earth's fever. Dung that would have otherwise been poured into waters that would thereafter suffer from abundance. We have kept a count of what we've taken from earth to build New Sky World, because we have a responsibility to give it back."

"Even the dung?" one of the littlest children asked, interrupting, sounding skeptical in the way that only small children can.

"Even the dung," Moth replied with a chuckle. "Every molecule of matter that has been taken from Earth and set among the stars is remembered and missed by the earth. Much of humankind for the last few hundred years has given little thought, if any, to the ethics of taking matter from Earth with no intent to return it. But to reap without sowing is called 'extractivism' and it is one of the most harmful parts of the sickness called 'capitalism'. We must be mindful not to repeat the mistakes of others. When we'd coaxed enough life into the soil, we began to invite and introduce other beings—worms and springtails and mites, insects and complex plants. It was many years before we could begin planting trees and introducing big animals. But it was because we followed the earth's lead that we succeeded where others failed. Humankind cannot and should not live without other beings. It's easy to understand why we need deer and turkeys, and why they need woodlands and meadows. It's harder, for people who don't understand or care about the complicated relationships between beings, to understand that we also need beavers and groundhogs, wolves and bears, hummingbirds and butterflies, asters and goldenrod. Why we need to include mosquitos and ticks, even if we quarrel with them. Our world is the only place where some creatures live, right now. The northern long-eared bat, the blue-spotted salamander, the American burying beetle. We hope, someday, that the earth becomes well enough to harbor these creatures again. We hope that we are living with the ancestors of the ones that will go home."

"When will Earth be better?" another child asked.

"Healing takes as long as it takes," Moth said, evenly. "It was the work of generations for the earth to become sick, and it will be the work of generations for it to become well again. Those of our people who stayed on Earth are working there to preserve and restore. Some of you might go there to learn, someday, just as people from earth come here to learn about New Sky World."

"Our marine biology teacher, Sokeenun, lives on Earth," a child said. "She lives on Nonamesset Island, at a research station. We have 'net classes with her."

Moth might have said something else, but the phone in her pocket buzzed. She took it out to find a new text from Maykitu-ash. Her face lit up with a smile as she read,

'Don't mean to interrupt I know you're with kids but they're carving the maple-smoked poskáttuck so maybe come back to the meetinghouse?'

"Supper's ready," Moth relayed to the children, tucking her phone back into her pocket. "Somebody help me stand up, my old knees are tired."

She did not want for helpers, and all together they walked back to the village proper, where the others were talking and laughing, singing and dancing and enjoying good food, sharing stories of their own.

Imprint

Cheyenne Dakota Williams

You greeted the lightning in your language
and all I could think about was how I was taught
to run away from these things—to evade the percussion
of thunder with tetrad utters for reasons that are still
unknown.

I seem to have inherited a maternal neurosis
in which my lineage states matriarchs must uphold
tradition—I do not say this in good providence
for I can't think of an ancestress whom I truly
admire.

Despite my best efforts to endure flames,
sparks inroad the parts of my soul
faltering against an extinguished
future—Can you blame me? It starts
on the count of three.

My adobe heart believed your tribal endonym
would indicate an instinctive appellation—
that perhaps the domain of your quinate shores
could harbor my maroon flames; a salve for my desert
droughts.

I'm envious of those that can manage their vernacular.
My throat is too meek—won't you kiss me into fluency?
My guttural palate was scrubbed clean into a repressed leash.

Your dialect fascinates me, so I search for the flavor of words
down your throat.

My hair will grow longer, and I'll wear an updo in homage
to women in a picture I saw—a glimpse you will never get.
I'll drink the cordial brew harvested on the side of highways,
the herbs boiling on the stove, and I will finally tell you
what the taste meant.

It was the repulsion of your kiss. The foggy fragrant
whirled me into its reproach, a brume of ruminations cupped
me of all that I have lost—more pours out tomorrow. My
tongue
blistered from each acrid sip, as my throat spit out the last of
your bitter residue.

Toppenish

Maritza N. Estrada

145

My memory holds no tender age moments of this town. I once read it's *Where the West Still Lives.* A city of murals of brown and white portraits, casitas, and wild horses. When my mother picked this town, she said it was quiet and had friendly folk. Then, I was born. As of the 2020 census, the city's population is 8,854 and is within the Yakama Nation. I visited twenty-three years later with a camera, abuelita, and my father in a Nissan. The valley greeted us and I thought, *I existed here.* The wind waved outside the window with wonder. My mother had said before, *If we had stayed, our lives would have been different.* Years later, I learned it was people who made a city home. When I stepped outside the car and snapped the hospital, muted mountains, and mobile homes, I read a distant sign, stating ROAD CLOSED TO THE PUBLIC EXCEPT BY PERMIT FROM THE YAKAMA TRIBAL COUNCIL ACTION WILL BE BROUGHT AGAINST ALL VIOLATORS, and thought, *Yes, mhmm* before we turned around back to Grandview to the local Burger Ranch for some asparagus fries, burgers, and Washington sauce.

A love letter to the land

Pte San Win Little Whiteman

If you could write a love letter to the land, what would you say?

I'm not sure.

I don't think words are enough to describe
my deep appreciation for all she's done—
I guess
I'd ask her how she does it.

How does she continue to make the trees and flowers grow,
or allow the sun to rise,
even after all that has happened to her.

I'd ask her for a hug because her resiliency must be tiring.

I'd ask her to smudge because when I do,
I feel less heavy,
and maybe if she does,
the stars will sing,
and the stars
will cry to the moon about what it's like to breathe.

I'd ask her about the rocks,
and if she feels as strong as they.

I'd ask about the pain,
and where it hurts the most.
I'd grab my bundle of cedar and sage,
And when I'm done asking,
I'd tell her about my scars,
and how they still hurt too.

I'd tell her *Thehicila na Pilamaya.*

Thank You and I Love You.

Observatory Regard

Maritza N. Estrada

Verde tequila, mother mezcal, each weekend
weakened, my manzana-mazed heart—

the lover watching of an honored appreciation study.

I have grown an apple tree for a selected kind;
twenty-five ongoing to twenty-six years; verde manzana mid-air

between the stillness from stem to branch;
manzana mid-air between the lover's shoulders,

& every tense you hold the chi-breast, I anchor
myself underground, root-field, ruthlessly

naming you by -co, chi-co, chi-co—.

Hold the apple w/ those godly hands;
root-veins, one I grown & grown:

Your hips are beautiful, the hands mapped,
wide for children—a plurality I vision until then,

am in search for the soles of feet to rim
of head, we build this tree in & in & in—

I have gardened of search for my counterpart,
silent & observingly.

Hold the lover's hand to enter within an apple's core.
& it rained for one hundred years after because it had been fed.

So many manzana fields outgrew the thing
they couldn't name.

homecoming

Samah Serour Fadil

my mother read my poem to me and it felt like a breeze the staccato of her english telling me i could breathe every sylla-ble pushing every word a war on her tongue but she rested in the trenches & spent time with each one her voice rolled back in & she nodded in agreement with every line & i felt so many emotions within me rise & when the last word left her war torn mouth the tears forming behind my eyes left mine unspooling everything inside in the end all i had to give was on the page she called me an artist wondered why i'd never come to her why i'd never shown this to her i said the only poetry you ever read was written by God how could i fathom offering you these mortal words what i offer instead is eternal love & it forms in these let-ters, this is my offering, all I have is this poem.

Signal from Noise

Andrea L. Rogers

"A bad time's coming and I want to be far away. I don't think that's crazy." The young woman spoke with an assurance the doctor mistrusted immediately. Her outgrown black bangs waved out and over her eyes like a battered awning, the top of her tortoiseshell glasses were mostly hidden.

Maggie's mother had made the appointment for her, requesting that her mental health be evaluated. The school counselor had called her at work, insinuated that protective services would be called in should no action be taken. "Maggie must be seen by a professional before she returns to school," the counselor had said.

"Maggie, *crazy* is the word I would prefer we not use. No one is suggesting that. Your mom seemed really worried." The psychiatrist allowed his spectacles to slide down his nose. Maggie wanted to reach over and push them up, the way her mother did when Maggie was reading on the couch.

"She's afraid they'll take me away." Maggie glanced up at the diplomas and certifications on the wall, solidly geographically Texan. The math had him actively shrinking less than eight years. Maggie wondered if he knew if he had even met an Indian before. *He's probably a post ICWA baby*, she thought. Is unaware that the breaking up of Native families was an historic solution to the Indian problem.

"The school only wants what's best for you. Why do you think they are worried?" He made a note on the tablet.

"You mean afraid." The office smelled of new paint and carpet, not like the urgent cares in the backs of drugstores where she usually saw doctors.

"Why do you think they would be afraid? Are you a danger to yourself or others?"

Maggie rolled her eyes. "No. I don't want to hurt anyone. Me included. That's why I think we should leave the city. Mom is afraid. She wants to believe all the bad things coming are the normal bad things. Isn't that funny? Like some bad things are acceptable? Others are not?"

"Most things exist on a spectrum. A cold is bad, but other things are worse. It's hardly a binary."

Maggie shrugged.

"So, Maggie, what makes you think a bad time is coming? Did someone tell you this? Was it in something you read or watched on the computer?"

Maggie closed her eyes. She seemed to be weighing whether to speak. She looked out the window, toward the zoo that was a half mile north of the office building and fifteen floors down. She stood up and tried to see the park, the taller trees swaying in the wind, the green expanse a mirage of peace. Finally, like anyone who has been burdened with a secret for too long, the words began.

"Do you know what the crush box is?"

The doctor made a note on their tablet. "I can't say that I do."

"You know how intelligent elephants are, right? They cry. They love. They have culture and rituals and memory."

"Yeah?"

"You ever see those elephants with people riding on them?"

"Yes. We did that at a zoo once, when I was a kid. I have a picture somewhere."

"Elephants have to be trained to tolerate that. When they are young, they are taken from their mothers. They are put in a cage and beaten with whips and bull hooks for twenty-four hours. It's desensitization. They are taught to fear man more than they trust their mothers. If they come out of the box and run to their mothers, they get put back in the box again and again for more beating. They are taught to ignore their instincts, to ignore the sounds of their mother's cry, to ignore the pressure on their soft parts."

"I didn't know. That's really awful." He made a note on his tablet.

"We do that, too."

"What do you mean?"

"We learn to ignore the pain of the world. We walk past people sleeping on sidewalks. Dogs chained up. People who are lonely."

"So, you can hear these messages of pain? Do you mean other people or animals or…"

"I just feel it. It's in the way the birds talk when they think no one is listening. It's in the dogs barking at each other. It's in the way the strays in the alley slink away when I surprise them. They don't act frightened anymore. They seem like they are biding their time."

The doctor made another note on his pad and waited. To a person with lots to say silence is better than a question.

"If you look in the papers or read those strange news bits on the internet, you can see a pattern emerging. There are battles going on every day. They are killing us, and we are killing them." She stopped and corrected herself. "No, we torture them before we kill them. People started it. Their indifference to the feelings and lives of the world's flora and fauna."

"Who are we torturing?"

Maggie frowned and sat tensely on the edge of the seat. She worried that she'd said too much. She was unable to take it back but afraid to go on. His clinical concern felt observational.

"Maggie," the doctor said softly, "who is killing us?"

"Obviously, they haven't killed us. And I haven't killed them. But it's going on out there. Every day you read about it. Two dogs attack elderly woman in her yard. Deer attacks hunter. Child throws kitten from an overpass. Dog owners find missing poodle skinned. If it's horrible it has happened to an animal." Maggie looked out the window again. "I think the earth and the animals have had enough."

Her voice rushed on. "I mean there are anomalies. Small dog fights to protect owner from two strays. Woman risks life to save family pet. Those are aberrations. We hear and see awful stuff. Think about all the awful stuff we don't hear. It seems like kindness was once a norm. Now it's headline news."

"And the animals have told you about this? They have let you know that they have had enough?"

Maggie sucked in a breath instead of answering.

"You know about the collective consciousness, right?"

"The idea that all humans share a culture, drink from the same pool of thought?"

"Well, imagine that the collective is a broadcast, a two-way radio but all you have is a microphone. You're constantly broadcasting your intentions, your desires, your secrets. Every little, ooh, I'd like to eat that last piece of cheesecake and wow, aren't they good looking? But also, your moods emanate in a kind of white noise that varies in pitch and intensity. People mostly think in words because we depend on speech to communicate but some of our communication is nonverbal. So, why couldn't animals broadcast, too?"

"So, you can hear the animals' broadcast?" The doctor was writing quickly, only looking up now and then.

Maggie sighed audibly this time. "No, animals don't speak the way we do so I couldn't understand them if I could hear them anyway. If I heard French, I wouldn't be able to understand much of it, either. My point is that we know animals communicate without speech, so they are less limited in the reception of the broadcast. They have a microphone and an antenna. We just yammer with our monkey mind microphone and don't listen. At least not on a conscious level." Maggie was speaking out loud thoughts she had never shared with anyone else before.

"Okay." She paused, searching her mind for an example. "Two weeks ago on the radio, I heard a story about dolphins. Researchers asked them to come up with a routine and perform it to obtain a reward. The dolphins looked at each other, made no audible noises, and then proceeded to perform an original routine. They understood the human's request and they decided on a sequence, without talking—at least talking as we think of it."

The doctor made a note to himself to look the story up.

"So, you hear these things?"

Maggie was visibly frustrated. "I told you, I don't speak dolphin or dog or polar bear. It's static. It's radio waves. It's digital cable and all I have are a pair of rabbit ears. But it has a nuance. There is anxious white noise and there is happy white noise. And the white noise I keep hearing is building and it's not happy. The city is going to be a bad place soon. I want to be gone before then."

The phone the doctor was using to record the session buzzed on the table, suddenly, and the doctor jumped. It wasn't often a patient unnerved him. It was amazing what people could believe.

"My apologies," he said, ticking the phone to do not disturb after glancing at it.

When the session was over, Maggie's mom was in the waiting room. She and Maggie changed places, Maggie sitting down to wait for her, her mom in the psychiatrist's office.

"What did she tell you?"

"She believes bad things are going to happen. To humans. A battle between us and animals, maybe?"

Maggie's mom nodded. "She really believes it?"

"It would seem so. Has she had any other strange behavior? Do you think she's a danger?"

"No. I just needed to know she believed it enough to tell someone else."

"We have space at the psychiatric facility. Without more testing, it's hard to know whether or not she's hallucinating. It sounds like she is. Why don't we send her over there for the week of observation? Prescribe some antipsychotics?"

Maggie's mom shook her head.

The doctor made a note, frowning. "Well, then shall we schedule for next week?"

Maggie's mom shook her head again and stood up. "You'll bill me?"

"Well, I think it would be a good idea to start regular appointments. The school counselor would look favorably on that."

"Sure. Same time next week?"

The doctor nodded. "Your insurance isn't very comprehensive. There'll be a hundred-dollar copay. You'll be charged whether you show up or not."

Maggie's mom pressed her lips together, gently nodding. Not daring to talk.

Neither Maggie nor her mom spoke, but they walked close, Maggie's mom's arm threaded through hers for the long walk across the heated blacktop.

"You smell smoke?" Maggie asked.

They had reached the car and her mom was distracted. She stopped going through her purse long enough to sniff the air.

"It's been so dry," she said, unlocking the car.

Maggie opened the backdoor to stow away her backpack. The seat was piled with suitcases and bags and blankets.

"What's up with all the stuff, mom?" When it was only the two of them, Maggie didn't hide her fear.

"I thought maybe it was a good time to get out of the city. Visit your grandma in Tulsa."

From a few rows over, a car alarm trumpeted, startling them

both. At the zoo, half a mile away, an elephant responded, their cry a question and call.

In the car's front seat, Maggie hugged herself. "Tulsa is a city, too, Ma."

"Yeah, but it's surrounded by the rez, now, and that's a start."

Maggie laughed. Her mom turned towards her and didn't seem to know what to do with her hands.

Maggie leaned her head onto her mom's shoulder. Her mom pulled her into a good hug, strong and gentle.

Maggie hugged her mom back just as hard.

Kahilinā'i

Ha'åni Lucia Falo San Nicolas

My first sister in O'ahu bears
defiant black curls, coiled as
tight as her conviction. Like

me, she is here for graduate
school, but she tells me that
Honoka'a is home, the 'āina

where coqui frogs, native to
Puerto Rico, break day for the
mana of Mauna a Wakea, the

sacred summit and ancestor of
Kanaka Maoli, her lāhui. We
met in the virtual realm of

online classes, but my na'au
reminds me that she and I are
wound in pilina, related by our

piko: our shared being as
women of the Pacific. I knew
you long before I learned your

name because I was raised by
Mongmong, a village titled
after the beating sound of

the heart—
mong mong mong
mong mong mong

and although coqui here are not
as loud as they once were, I am
greeted at dawn by Guåhan, the

land where CHamorus descend
from. As wahine and palao'an we
are connected at the navel of our

ocean, who brings you and I together
again. We are far from our roots, but
on a yellow Post-it wedged between

a gifted copy of *Iep Jaltok: Poems from
a Marshallese Daughter*, she graces me
with story:

> Ha'åni,
> island to island to island
> an ever-growing constellation.

I learned weeks after we parted
ways that her name, Kahilinā'i,
means the one to trust, believe, and

rely upon. When we find comfort
and love and friendship in one
another, we give life to our piko.

Splice of Genetic Material

Amelia Vigil

my origins
a void
supernova's long spark
an egg that split
our duality in human form
these bones
these bones
the tightrope of exile
our history a road called forgetting
Pura Pecha/ Mexica mother
Spanish Sephardic /Picuris Father
coated Xicano
hard candy racial casting
these bones
these bones
we forget are made of light
are made of used protons
we the split threads
fibers refortified
by our fuzzy reform
a twenty-year long weekend
a five-point bent at queer, quick, wit, quirky tips
a splice genetic material
hair, eyes
teeth, throat
these bones
these bones

are on loan

Beyond the Glittering World

Shaina A. Nez

WITCHES

The first time I read *Storyteller* by Leslie Marmon Silko, I got chills reading about the witches coming together for a show-and-tell night. It was midnight, and I was up reading in my dorm room alone one weekend. I couldn't sleep. That night, I twisted my body to its right side and tried closing my eyes to slumber, but I could only picture the lone witch reciting its story of colonization. I remember nalí reciting a shorter version of a time he had followed a witch by horseback, and the thing hidden in a heap of sagebrush, hoping he would leave. But nalí waited until it showed itself in the pale moonlight; four days later, someone in the community passed away for reasons unknown. I never thought I would see a witch in its truest form.

I looked back at this story and wondered about witches in their truest form—they could be everywhere, and our spirit had to be protected. No one discussed witches in stories anymore; we wrote in fear, careful not to violate Native and Indigenous ethical practices of story. But that didn't mean the evil wasn't lurking, waiting to strike another innocent relative. And no one talked about how witches transformed to keep their teachings alive—you heard about them as scouts, those who joined the cavalry to narc on their own people with no shame or remorse that they turned their backs almost immediately for special treatment. They would never understand their own destruction of the people who still cared about them—the ones who cared will still die from the bones of witches, with love pulsating in their hearts.

WEEK ONE

Thirteen years passed, and I was teaching my first college-level fiction class. As the many faceless bodies entered the room, finding their spaces for the rest of the semester, a woman appeared wearing onyx shades so dark I could see my outline staring back at me. I welcomed everyone to the introductory class, and we began learning about each other and the books we would read during the semester. I was back at my alma mater, ready to teach the next generation of voices who wanted to tell stories from the beauty of their bellies, I told them, because they would learn about Native and Indigenous epistemologies in story, both now and then.

It was midnight and I was grading a batch of introduction essays written as statements of purpose. My first assignment to the fiction students was to introduce themselves and their relationships with writing and reading fiction. I loved hearing about some of the new Native authors and poets they were sharing and some of their favorite fiction titles, until I came across Black Shades' submission. She had not talked about Native authors or poets; instead, she had described her intimate, delicate relationship with splatterpunk fiction, a genre that centered characters who felt confined by the norms and expectations of society and who broke free of those confines in unusual or illicit ways. She wrote in verse and much like a colonial white man. I thought back to my first day in the classroom, thinking of her sitting in the back corner and what she shared about herself with us. She had spoken with a distinct voice, almost song-like, and when she shared her nation and name, she had not used her Native dialect. The books she shared were titles like *We Prey We Pray*, *The Nowhere Women*, and *Fatal Fear*. My first impression of her introduction essay was the fluidity in her writing—she had not been caught between the past and present tenses, she displayed mature language for a freshman, and her voice carried confidence. I was pleased that she hadn't shared similar titles as her classmates, and maybe I could teach her an appreciation for contemporary Native and Indigenous authors as a starting place.

FEAR

In addition to building an appreciation for what we read, I included in the course syllabus supplemental readings by Matthew Salesses, *Craft in the Real World: Rethinking Fiction Writing and Workshopping*, for those unfamiliar with writing workshop structure and history. I believed in building up this introduction to fiction in all aspects that would shape and frame their minds to view Other stories and help them begin their firsts without fear of failure or ridicule, the kind I once faced during my time earning a writing degree. I am a millennial educator, of course, raised on silence first and the notion of not asking questions, of not nibbling on the hands that fed you—in a sense of the writing world. But then came decolonial thought, which raised concerns for Native and Indigenous writers who thrived on story for its cutthroat honesty, only to be nurtured and cared for, like how we do in our communities. I am an activist raised on heartwork and teaching with a focus on justice. The students were expected to explore stories as earnest and untold, uncomfortable truths with needed elaboration. Fear, to me, meant overcoming challenges face-on, like nalí, who waited to stare down the witch in its truest form. We needed those stories of hope.

FOUR R'S

We were in week five, beginning our first round of critiquing our creative fictional work. After reading a couple of stories by Stacie Denetsosie and Chelsea T. Hicks, I assigned the students to write a story capturing beauty in whatever they saw. They didn't need to focus on point of view just yet, or even story structure—a first draft was meant to be shitty, I joked. Everyone shared the humor, except for Black Shades. I noticed she wore these spectacles every Tuesday and Thursday, but this wasn't high school with a dress code, so I never mentioned taking them off during class. As I tilted my head to face hers, I couldn't tell if she was staring back—but she beamed a smirk. I thought maybe she just needed more time to ease up. Some Native students could match your energy with a good joke, others stayed quiet on purpose, and some just needed space to pause their hyper-sensitivities and let loose. During the workshop, a student wrote about teenagers forming a punk rock band in rebellion against the No Child Left Behind Act of 2001—raised by the presidency of George W. Bush—and touring across the Navajo Nation singing of beauty. I praised the story's attempt at a transformational stage in the plot and its giving toward an "Indigenous Futurism" sort of vibe. Everyone except for Black Shades gave positive feedback; she, however, decided to go for the kill, telling the writer it was a weak storyline of hope and that reservation teenagers were not a 'real' eclectic mix of musicians. I immediately stopped her from saying more and asked her to take a breath, to go for a walk and cool down. She jerked up from her chair; it flipped over dramatically as she exited the classroom.

Hush.

I reassured the classroom that these outbursts could happen in workshop. But because we stated our workshop was a safe space, she had to channel her fuming energy elsewhere. I ended class a little early. On a positive note, the story sparked strong feelings about rebellion in the community and that from a justice standpoint, our youth deserved to be heard, honored, and praised for their creative expression evoking beauty. When Black Shades returned with a little bounce in her step, I asked her to sit down. She sat at her desk in the back corner, and it was only her and me in the naturally lit classroom.

I approached her gently, wanting to get a better understanding. "You look bothered during workshop. Is something going on?" I asked.

She responded with a shrug in her tone. "I wasn't trying to tear her piece apart. I was just being honest about how I felt. It wasn't meant to come off like I thought her writing was bad."

"That's not what you said," I reminded her. "You mentioned the storyline lacked strength when it came to portraying hope."

She tried to brush it off. "Yeah, but upsetting her wasn't my intention."

I kept my voice steady. "Do you remember the four R's we said would guide how we hold space in workshop?"

She let out a laugh at the question, but I shifted my tone—calm no longer, firm and serious now. The humor drained from her expression, replaced by the familiar look of discomfort she had shown when I asked her to step out earlier.

She inhaled, then recited, "Respect, Responsibility, Reciprocity, and Relationships."

I didn't let up. "And what do those mean?"

She groaned, nearly raising her voice. "Seriously?"

I stood from my desk, picked up a dry-erase marker, and extended it toward her. "Then show me. Write it out."

When she finished, she stood next to me and we read the capital letters in front of us silently:

1. RESPECT: WE RESPECT ONE ANOTHER'S INQUIRIES, WRITING STAGES, AND PROCESSES.

2. RESPONSIBILITY: WE LEARN ABOUT OUR RESPONSIBILITIES AS WRITERS.

3. RECIPROCITY: WE WILL RECIPROCATE LOVE, MOTIVATION, AND SUPPORT ON GOOD AND BAD DAYS.

4. RELATIONSHIPS: WE WILL BUILD A DEEP APPRECIATION AND REGARD FOR OUR RELATIONSHIPS BECAUSE THEY MATTER.

I turned to her, and we were standing nearly eye to eye. At that closer distance, I notice the acne scars on the sides of her face, the sandstone shade of her skin that curved just so, and the black shades now more visible. I could almost make out the shape of her eyes. They looked almond-like, but they were bubbly at the center. As she shifted her back leg, shadows tucked away the outline of her gaze. Somehow, the mood and energy in the room changed. She repeated her apology, said she would commit to the four R's of the workshop, and added she would also apologize to the student by email and copy me on it. Her voice softened here as she shuffled away from my sight and out of the classroom. She sent the email to her peer in less than twenty minutes. I could tell she had gone to the library to complete this task—an acknowledgement of her faults, and a step toward learning how to nourish the stories of others during workshop.

GREED

During Black Shades' critique, everyone showered her story with love, and she hoarded the praise with a kind of greed, hiding behind her ebony spectacles. When a student asked if the woman in the story was truly beaten and jumped by five men, Black Shades replied that it had not happened in real life. At that moment, I was sitting in my advanced fiction class back in undergrad, remembering how our instructor and many other fiction experts often repeated: A fictional story is told through a mask, and you would never know what is real and what is not; what the author gives is a matter of trust. I believed Black Shades lied to her peer during workshop, and what I later uncovered about this story was that she had lured this character into the hands of these resentful men, for reasons that remained unknown. The class never learned what happened to the woman later in the story's development.

INDIGENOUS' PEOPLES WEEK

It had been Indigenous Peoples' Week, a time I liked to practice celebrating the real history of the Americas. I assigned an extra credit opportunity for the students to read "Tony's Story" by Leslie Marmon Silko and "The Killing of a State Cop" by Simon Ortiz. I figured that since it was the spirit of Halloween, the students would appreciate chilling tales and understand how writers researched factual information using newspaper archives. We had been building a timeline of stories, and I had kept the intention of literary appreciation mixed with the works of foundational writers in dark, horror, and Native fiction. The students were to write a response essay about the two stories and share in their conclusion what potential stories they could write and what history from their own community they could explore. They could research the local paper's archives online as a starting point later in the unit.

At midnight, I had been grading the extra credit essays and learning about the students' inquiries. Before reading the stories, they based their speculation on the titles alone and wrote whether their assumptions held any merit. When it came to Black Shades' submission, she disliked the two stories, arguing that the Native men had broken the law and should have been imprisoned for the rest of their lives for killing a state trooper. I anticipated that her elaboration would further tomorrow's discussion.

In class, I warned the students that we would discuss some topics openly that other Native writers formed various opinions about: witchcraft. During this discussion, a student raised the theme in Silko's story, first talking about the state cop who struck Leon repeatedly at the community fair. Another student chimed in, referencing Silko's description of the dark glasses the officer wore. Then, a student in the group whispered a little too loudly that the imagery of sunglasses reminded her of Black Shades. The classroom had gone dead silent for a split second, and I realized Black Shades was not in class; she missed that day of discussion. I then reminded the class of the four R's, both in and out of workshop, and urged them to remain courteous and professional. I was disappointed knowing she wasn't there. I had been hoping to hear her controversial opinions about the dangerous narratives these stories painted between the state police that helped keep Native communities safe and when we couldn't solely rely on the tribal police force. Her conclusion stated she would research similar crimes but write from a perspective of retributive justice. Her opposing viewpoint gave the students in the classroom a chance to push back on thoughts, and I planned to give her kudos for that. Nonetheless, Silko's version had truly challenged the narrative of justice for the brothers versus the witch cop, who appeared to be racist, intimidating, and likely had a background history of roughing up minoritized POC when police brutality hadn't yet been named.

Later that night, I tossed and turned in my bedroom and finally dozed off until I imagined Black Shades standing at the edge of my bed, holding a long bone at me, just like how Antonio was described in Silko's story. I opened my eyes into the darkness and saw nothing.

BLUE EYES

Midterm week has passed, and grades were posted. That's how I seem to keep track of time, at least during the academic year. As I sat back at my office desk, I looked out the window and noticed how the brisk coolness of fall changed the landscape. A knock at the door, and I turned in my seat to see Black Shades and a colleague I hadn't met, standing together, waiting to be let in.

"Hi!" I gestured at the empty seats. "Please come sit down." The colleague smiled now and took his seat, and Black Shades said nothing but followed suit. "What can I do for you?" I asked.

The unknown colleague brought up the topic of midterm grades and gestured toward Black Shades, indicating that she was not pleased with her grade. Suddenly, I wondered about the true intention of this visit. Grades had already been posted. I clarified, "You're asking me to change her grade?"

"If that's not too much trouble," he replied.

"Actually…it is," I said, looking at Black Shades. "I preferred she take the grade as is." I now wondered why we were suddenly referring to this student in the third person—and why wasn't she making this request herself?

"Ok…" the colleague smiled, as if he gave the final word. They rose from their seats, with only him saying goodbye, and they departed. I closed my office door after them and decided to think nothing more of that particular visit—perhaps Black Shades had not been honest with Professor X about this request, and the colleague now understood the mishap.

The following week, I received an email from the same colleague asking me to join him for lunch at a nearby café. I had not met the rest of my colleagues yet—only by Zoom, if that counted—so I took this invitation as an effort to bring me up to speed with the program as a new faculty hire. I replied that I was free, and we exchanged phone numbers.

As we took our seats in the Owl Café, he asked if the place was against my culture, chuckling at his question. "It's fine," I said, knowing damn well others would find it offensive. But I didn't say anything—because I didn't know this person yet, and I was still trying to.

While the server took our food and beverage orders, I took in the colleague's physical features. He was clean-cut with strawberry blonde hair, a narrow face shape, and blue eyes, and had been teaching at the college for almost a decade. He mentioned "doing work" for Native communities, and I wondered why he came off as mocking it. Every time he brought up Native communities, it had to end with some kind of humor. Trust me, humor often brings POC groups and individuals together—essentially to laugh at our pain and poke fun at it—but when non-POC individuals do this, I question whether it was a potential mind game.

"Whatever you do," my former MFA mentor said when she heard the news about my first teaching job, "do not let your colleagues play any mind games with you. Academia is a war zone; tread carefully. And if someone tries to power play you, don't back down. We need more women in this field to rid these spaces of the dominant male energy. I'm proud of you. You got this."

Her words rang in my temple, and a red flag emoji practically hovered above his head anytime his tone of voice elevated. Suddenly, he shifted the topic and began asking about Black Shades—how she was doing in my class. I told him she was doing well. He pushed back, saying maybe not well enough if she had a B at midterms. I chuckled at his comment and replied, "Oh, same difference." His smile vanished, then he tried to recover with laughter, but I already noticed the reaction. I now understand that this lunch was only a negotiation tactic for Black Shades' midterm grade. Again. My exit plan kicked in: eat fast, thank him for the meet-up, and bolt.

NOWHERE LAND

The students were wrapping up studio/independent time, finishing their research and drafting—practicing how to flesh out a story, as they put it. *Don't worry about being grammatically correct here*, I had told them. *Just keep your character's agency at the forefront of your stream of consciousness.* By the end of the day, everyone submitted a workable draft—except Black Shades. She asked for an extension and promised to turn in the draft next class, but I told her no. I asked what she had been doing during the independent time. She didn't reply. I told her to submit whatever she had, at least for attendance. She ripped out a page from her notebook and handed me a single sheet. I turned it over and scanned the details. She had written her name, the class info, the date, and centered the capitalized title of her new story—NOWHERE LAND—but there was no story. Before I could say anything, she was already out the door. On Thursday, Black Shades placed a freshly printed out of NOWHERE LAND on my desk, ten minutes before class started. She sat waiting for the rest of her peers to come in, visibly pleased with herself. I didn't acknowledge the submission right away, sticking to the lesson plan. After class, I asked her to stay back and pull up a chair to my desk. We sat across from each other, and she kept a poker face. I asked her to explain the story to me—give me a verbal synopsis. *Paint me a picture. What should I expect when reading this?* She said it was a fanfiction piece based on *The Nowhere Women.* I pushed her to think more critically about the protagonist. She stared downward, her frame tensing. She described the heroine, Lucy, as an only child raised by her grandmother after the tragic death of her parents. Lucy was curious about sex, sexuality, and substances, but made it clear that Lucy was sober. The curiosity, Blake Shades said, came from stories she'd heard about her parents partying, and from her circle of friends.

The friend group sounded like bad seeds, but she made a point—they were from the same community, and Lucy was honoring their destructiveness as a means of survival.

I asked her more about *The Nowhere Women*, specifically if there were other titles like it. That one question lit up her whole aura—or at least what I could see, since her shades still covered most of her face.

"Yes," she said. "You should read *We Prey We Pray.*" It came out like a demand, but she caught herself and added, "Please."

Maybe this is a breakthrough? I nodded and agreed to read it.

Then we talked—talked about the injustices in Native communities that make up a tribal nation. We broke down social statuses, elitism, and how injustice continues even when money, support, and resources are supposedly there. We justified why some people advance and others don't, why support doesn't always reach those it's meant for, and how that affects the growth of our professionals.

That side conversation gave me a fuller picture of this student's integrity. She seemed to have a good head on her shoulders, just clouded by the mainstream ideologies of writers who don't prioritize community or kinship.

At midnight, I was lying back on the sofa, reading *We Prey We Pray*. Beyond all the violence and heinous imagery—bloodied bodies, stabbings, and penetration—I concluded that the main character, Andrew, was obsessed with power and control, and wanted all of it to share with his true lover, who was, in fact, a living, breathing mare. I didn't judge the book, nor did I judge her taste in fiction. With my deconstruction goggles on, the blood and guts became secondary. This could easily be a story about a mediocre man who had no real agency in life and tried to assert it onto the livelihood of mares.

Oh geez. I thought back to all the stories of yt saviors and found myself now judging the underlying message.

NOWHERE LAND was written in first person, and the characters from Black Shades' earlier workshop draft were present in this version too. The more deeply I read, the more the moral of the violence attempted to surface. A girl who had been beaten was now exchanging text messages with the protagonist about the incident—but there was no mention of how the victim was feeling.

The final text message in the scene read: *you wanted their attention, you wanted change, but now you know this cycle never stops.*

I cringed.

As I Googled other titles Black Shades had listed in her introduction essay, I noticed how men were consistently centered in these stories, while the women were treated ghastly—like Eve, sinners all over again, being ridiculed for their curiosities, for reaching toward forbidden fruit.

I found myself feeling sorry for Black Shades because she didn't even seem to realize that she was centering yt men, not reading between the lines, not noticing that women—specifically Native women—were being silenced. And this violent storytelling was perpetuating that erasure.

The story didn't need saving from a yt male-dominated lens. It needed saving from Leslie Marmon Silko.

CALLBACK

Instead of continuing our independent writing journeys that week, I told the class we should revisit the rest of *Storyteller* and a particular poem about colonization. I asked them to rearrange our seating into a circle, mirroring our workshopping setup, and invited everyone to read a stanza aloud.

When it was Black Shades' turn, she read the line: *Set in motion now, set in motion by our witchery set in motion to work for us. They will take this world from ocean to ocean, they will turn on each other, they will destroy each other, up here in these hills they will find the rocks, rocks with veins of green and yellow and black. They will lay it across the world and explode everything.*

She let the next person continue, and I observed her reaction to reading those lines aloud. Her chest was rising and falling slowly; she placed her hands gently on the table in front of her.

As a group, we unpacked the stanzas, discussing the presence of colonization—what Silko was truly saying would happen once it arrived. And then I asked: *Can a story be called back? For the witches, no. But for us—here and now—can we call a story forward into the future?*

I posed that final question to the class in writing, asking them to submit their answers on my desk before leaving for the day.

After everyone had gone and I closed the door, I rummaged

through the submissions looking for Black Shades' response.

Her answer read:

Do I think a story can be called back? Maybe. I often wonder about the coming-of-age stories of my parents. I don't know them at all—only through my grandmother. If their stories could be called back, I would do it and go back with them to NOWHERE LAND. Can a story be called forward? No. But I am still here.

I reread her response more than once and spent the rest of the day thinking about the interconnectedness of story and storytelling.

FEAR

The writing director called for an emergency meeting regarding some grant endeavors we needed to apply for ASAP— her acronym of choice in emails when shit was hitting the fan. Once the host granted me access into the virtual space, we began with class introductions from all the faculty faces.

When it was my turn to introduce what I was teaching that semester, I was caught off guard when Blue Eyes—the colleague who had invited me to lunch—unmuted his microphone and immediately asked what the students were learning in my classroom.

I was happy he was asking and thought maybe, somewhere down the line we could collaborate on developing some course content. I summarized the students' introduction to Native American epistemologies in story, explained how we incorporated the four R's into our workshopping, and mentioned that they had read a short story from *Storyteller* by Leslie Marmon Silko and a short story from *Men on the Moon* by Simon Ortiz to learn about researching before writing.

I noticed the majority of floating heads in cyberspace nodding in approval—except for Blue Eyes.

He followed up by asking for the particular story title from

Ortiz, and I gave it instantly. No one said anything after that. Blue Eyes suggested in the future, I should reconsider my syllabus with only classical fiction.

I laughed thinking he was joking, but I didn't see him sharing the same humor as he had back at Owl Café.

"Oh, you meant that, I'm s—" I started, but before I could say sorry, another faculty member chimed in, saying, "She doesn't need the classics. We should be prioritizing Native and Indigenous stories—we're in a new time."

Everyone began reacting, thumbs up and hearts floating above their names.

When the meeting ended, I stepped out of my office to use the restroom and saw Blue Eyes walking straight toward me, a book in his hand.

WHITE-YT

The weekend finally arrive, and my fiancé had a special trip planned for us in the valley. I was reluctant to leave our home and the classroom behind—usually my sanctuary, was the office-home space where I could immerse myself into writing—but I needed to get away and clear my head. Ever since Blue Eyes visited my office, I had gotten chills every time I pictured him handing me that book. Instead of excusing myself to the restroom like I intended, I invited him to sit down, hoping he would talk fast. He apologized for interrupting my introduction during the meeting. It wasn't meant to be taken as a personal jab, he said. He knew my background in literature and trusted my future reading lists. His smile froze as he lifted his left arm, holding up a book and saying it should be a *joy to read*. He held up the book *We Prey We Pray* and told me it was a sweet book about life on a farm. I shook my head in disbelief and told him I already read it—because of Black Shades. The smile vanished from Blue Eyes. He tucked the book back under his arm and added, "I hope you loved it." I gave him my honest opinion about Andrew's character: that he was power-hungry, controlling, a coward for killing his mother and girlfriend, and imposing his colonized mindset onto the mares. Blue Eyes tried to minimize the violence against women, claiming they were purely evil and had no respect for Andrew. In defense of the genre, I agreed that Andrew's only answer was to kill—but from a justice lens, I argued he was a dissatisfied, middle-aged yt man, who struggled with his own sexuality and needed more than just an intervention; he needed someone to talk to like a couns—Blue Eyes cut me off. "He doesn't need counseling. He knows what he's doing—he is power-hungry and loves the mare named __________." In that moment, Blue Eyes didn't say Lisa, the name of Andrew's lover. He said Black Shades' full name. When he realized it, he laughed too loudly and blurted, "What am I saying? I didn't mean that," then apologized for intruding on my office hours and left in a flash. Before I could say anything, I noticed he had forgotten the book. I went to the restroom, freshened up, and decided to return the book back to his office. I headed down to the first floor, where Blue Eyes' office was. The door appeared closed. I was about to turn around, thinking I could just return the book on Tuesday, when I heard a giggle followed by muffled talking. It was a little after 5 p.m. No one else was around, and the aura turned eerie. I slowly approached his door, ready to knock—but it was open an inch. I peeked inside. Through the narrow view, I saw Blue Eyes and Black Shades sitting together. Her head rested on his shoulder. She looked comfortable. Her eyes were closed. The black spectacles were finally removed. Blue Eyes whispers something to her. She smiled and opened her eyes.

WHITE

YT EYEBALLS stared back at me.

__________ was looking right at me.

WEEK SIXTEEN

On the fourth day, I received an email from the writing director explaining that Blue Eyes was facing a personal matter and would not be returning for the rest of the academic year, effective immediately. They weren't sure if he would return at all based on the circumstances, but promised to keep us informed. In the meantime, she asked that if we know anyone who could take over his classes for the remainder of the year, we should send along contact information ASAP.

That same day, Black Shades didn't return to class. She didn't respond to my emails, and I informed the advisors at Student Affairs that she needed to be properly dropped from the course without receiving a 'W' on her official academic transcript. The advisor called me back and asked if I was sure that Black Shades had ever enrolled in my course. I asked why, and the advisor told me that, according to her college transcripts, she already completed an Introduction to Fiction course back in 2000, almost three decades ago.

Nalí's story and Silko's story warned me—and saved me— from a witch and a colonizer. What I knew now was that a witch can be anywhere, take any form, and that our spirits must remain protected at all costs—for the sake of our communities and teachings.

"Representation matters," I told the students on the last day of class. "And we should be honoring ourselves with love, compassion, and empathy anytime we put words down onto a page."

A CALL FORWARD

To the future beyond the Glittering World
There will be Black, Indigenous, all People of Color in this
world
Nothing will be European.
In the old world, there was witchery.
This world will be rid of witchery, beauty will be restored.

Set to come, we sing
Set to come by our beauty
to heal us all.

We will grow with the earth, the sun, with flora and fauna, and
we will honor life.
When we look around, we will see beyond wealth, greed, and fear.
The world is our mother, the sky is our father, and the water
and air are our children.
We will continue to honor our lives and the lives of others.
We will not choose to fear the world
We will bring peace, harmony, and autonomy.
We will stare fear in the eyes and pray for them to find their
chosen path.

Babies will smile a thousand sunbeams
Their happiness illuminates the land from darkness and shadows
Babies will laugh and move mountains
Ridding the structures of old caves where witches used to hide.

Set to come, we sing
Set to come by our beauty
to heal us all.

When earth, air, water, and fire come together
Together, they will rid us of diseases

Nations, cities, towns, and reservations will prosper
The land will cleanse itself from rocks with veins of green and
yellow and black
The pores and acne scars on Mother Earth will heal

Set to come, we sing
Set to come by our beauty
To heal us all
To restore
To pray
With pollen tongue
With sweetgrass
For the elders
For the parents
For the children
For everyone

Circle back
Circle back
a call forward
Set to come, we sing
Set to come by our beauty.

I call this story forward with love, compassion, and empathy
To the writing's future beyond the Glittering World.

Alfabetízate Otro Mundo: Reverse Abecedarian Broke Open

Ayling Dominguez

plea to all nonconformists to oppression: read EZLN comunicados

Zapatismo says to stop at no less than Un Mundo Donde
        Quepan Muchos Mundos. Until then,
yes, we are armed: with dreams and rifles,
xWaychinel Lum-K'inal.
Writing stories that begin with There Will Be a Time,
        not Once Upon.
Viendo y escuchando con el corazón, como bien dijo
        Comandanta Ramona.
Umbilical cord attachment style to the deep earth that birthed us,
to the weapon of resistance beating in the chests of everyone
deemed "other" and "different."
Sts'ikel vokol. The only thing we proposed was
to change the world, the rest* we have improvised.
*rebeldía/revolución/really, it all roots down to:
tierra y libertad must mean something to you,
        must mean everything to you.
The path to liberation gets wider the more of us tread it.
Que la lucha sea
para quienes se niega el día,
para quienes es regalo la muerte,
para quienes está prohibida la vida;

outrage is just as much our elder as hope is.
No model, no doctrine, no ideology, no blueprint,
          rather sacred intuition,
and mutuality, tools the master never had.
Landowners begone. The land rejects ownership
          from those who poison it.
Know that the government will try to discredit us,
          infiltrate us, kill us, but
jaguares y panteras negras know best how to remain
imaginative, thereby autonomous,
thereby alive.
Guardamos la flor de la palabra que viene desde el fondo de la
          historia y de la tierra.
From the mountains, always, the mountains,
          freedom feeds into the
ears of corn en las milpas, las calles, los zócalos;
          ears of tomorrow.
Descansa, Don Antonio, we are still dreaming
          the only dream that is dreamed awake.
Comrades, prepare yourselves. Keep your ocote on.
Below and to the left is where the heart is.
Aquí manda el pueblo.

If my love were a rez dog

Danielle Shandiin Emerson

Watch your heels, keep running,
gallup over dirt.
Kick dry weeds up as you skip, swinging
your arms from side to side,
swaying sunflowers
on the side of the ditch, where
we used to play as kids
until I almost drowned,
falling
deeper into cool spring water, listening to
lodged echoes of my name
and I thought, *Shandiin sounds beautiful
on your lips.*
There are so many translations:
Sunshine, sunlight, sunwarmth.
But my favorite comes from
when, at last,
you pulled me
up to the surface,
and I saw fierce honeydew
halo your wet hair, turning
your cheeks sheep white.
I thought, *Shandiin looks beautiful
on your face.*
If I were a rez dog, I'd keep chasing you.

Sunlight never stops
chasing you, it laps at your heels
and spreads like fresh watermelon juice
on your mouth and cheeks—puppy lidded kisses,
where moonlight secrets and fresh paw prints
almost feel all sacred—*nayee!*
Keep watching as our feet
hit the earth in a pitter-patter, a four-legged gallop
that elicits
sunshine, sunlight, sunwarmth,
honeydew.

To become a woman, whatever that is but I'm Navajo, so I have to know, especially now that I'm thirty-seven

Amber McCrary

Water mirror, my shell appears solemn
Who is this Asdzą́ą́ reflecting in the water—

Their sky is watching
They whisper *be a lesser deity*
Oh dear, an abalone anonymity—

an abalone wallpaper, blinding you with
my iridescent waves

Thirty-seven summers deep
the sun laughs at me
licks its cicatrix
and spits at me for kicks

She becomes an abalone asdzą́ą́
a woman learned to restrict
poker face in the reflection of coyotes

Abalone Asdzą́ą́ parks her shell by the sea,
others tell her how to be
and, how stubbornly, she rebels

Iridescent shell grazes membrane shallows
parked at the base of the mountain
to rest, laid on her side, for those
to call her Dookʼoʼoosłííd,

and we sing, like Kinsale and her sisters
driving through the night:
Don't go to sleep, Dookʼoʼoosłííd,
Don't go to sleep, Dookʼoʼoosłííd,
Don't go to sleep, Dookʼoʼoosłííd,

I turn my shell over
The ground is silent as pine needles

I bleed for its silence
Let me see and let me sleep

The sun laughs at me
and sings
Go to sleep, Bił nisin
Go to sleep, Bił nisin
Go to sleep, Bił nisin

My shell saunters on—

Contributors

MONIQUILL BLACKGOOSE is a Nebula Award-winning science fiction author, acclaimed for her bestselling novel *To Shape a Dragon's Breath*, the first in the now highly anticipated Nampeshiweisit series. An enrolled member of the Seaconke Wampanoag Tribe and a lineal descendant of Ousamequin Massasoit, Blackgoose began writing science fiction and fantasy at the age of twelve. She brings to life unique and diverse narratives, blending indigenous culture with rich fantasy elements. Her debut novel won the Andre Norton Nebula Award for Middle Grade and Young Adult Fiction.

STACIE SHANNON DENETSOSIE is an MFA graduate of the Institute of American Indian Arts and holds an MA from Utah State University. An enrolled member of the Navajo Nation, she is Todích'íí'nii (Bitterwater Clan), born for Naakaii (Mexican Clan). Originally from Kayenta, Arizona, she is the author of *The Missing Morningstar and Other Stories*, a PEN/Robert W. Bingham Prize finalist, a Southwest Book of the Year, a winner of the WILLA Literary Award, and a gold winner of the Foreword INDIES Award. She was named a 5 Under 35 honoree by the National Book Foundation in 2025. She lives in northern Utah with her husband and cat.

NATALIE DIAZ was born in the Fort Mojave Indian Village in Needles, California. She is Mojave and an enrolled member of the Gila River Indian community. She earned a BA from Old Dominion University, where she received a full athletic scholarship. Diaz played professional basketball in Europe and Asia before returning to Old Dominion to earn an MFA. She is the author of the poetry collections *Postcolonial Love Poem*, winner of the Pulitzer Prize, and *When My Brother Was an Aztec*. Her other honors and awards include the Nimrod/Hardman Pablo Neruda Prize for Poetry, the Louis Untermeyer Scholarship in Poetry from Bread Loaf, the Narrative Poetry Prize, and the Lannan Literary Fellowship.

AYLING ZULEMA DOMINGUEZ is a poet, educator, and community artist who dreams and writes toward a borderless world with rematriated lands. Their writing asks us to defy colonialism and nurture collective care in its place. Ultimately, they believe in poetry as dutiful imagination and liberation practice. Their storytelling is rooted in the lands of Puebla, México (Nahua) and the island of Kiskeya-Ayiti. Dominguez is a 2024–25 artistic development and teaching assistant at the Center for Imagination in the Borderlands, Arizona State University. Their poems have been published in *The Poetry Project*, *Yalobusha Review*, *Seventh Wave*, *The Texas Review*, *Huizache*, *Alebrijes Review*, *Beyond Borders Literary Review*, and elsewhere.

KINSALE DRAKE is a winner of the 2023 National Poetry Series for her debut poetry collection *The Sky Was Once a Dark Blanket*, a Southwest Book of the Year. She is Nat'oh Dine'é Tachiini, born for Bilagaana. Her maternal grandfather is Ashiihi, and her paternal grandfather is Bilagaana. She is a two-time winner of the Academy of American Poets University Prize and a former National Student Poet. Her work has appeared in *Poetry* Magazine, Poets.org, *Best New Poets*, *Black Warrior Review*, and elsewhere. She earned her BAs from Yale University and directs programming for NDN Girls Book Club, which distributes free books to Indigenous youth and communities. She currently lives in Nashville, Tennessee, as a graduate fellow at Vanderbilt University.

DANIELLE SHANDIIN EMERSON is a Diné writer from Shiprock, New Mexico on the Navajo Nation. Her clans are Tłaashchi'i (Red Cheek People Clan), born for Ta'neezaahníí (Tangled People Clan). Her maternal grandfather is Áshiihíí (Salt People Clan), and her paternal grandfather is Táchii'nii (Red Running into the Water People Clan). She has a BA in education studies and a BA in literary arts from Brown University. She has work published and/or forthcoming in *swamp pink*, Poets.org, *Yellow Medicine Review*, *Thin Air Magazine*, *Chapter House Journal*, and others. Her writing centers healing, kinship, language learning, and family. She is currently based in Bridgeport, Connecticut.

HEID E. ERDRICH's most recent poetry collection is *Verb Animate: Poetry and Prompts from Collaborative Acts*. Her honors include a National Poetry Series award, Native Arts and Cultures Foundation Fellowship, Loft-McKnight Fellowship in Prose, Minnesota State Arts Board grants, and two Minnesota Book Awards. Erdrich edited the anthology *New Poets of Native Nations*. Her poetry collection, *Little Big Bully*, won the Bobbitt Prize from the Library of Congress. She grew up in Wahpeton, North Dakota with a German American father, an Ojibwe and Métis mother, and six siblings. Erdrich is an enrolled member of the Turtle Mountain Band of Chippewa. She was the 2024 inaugural Minneapolis Poet Laureate and, in 2025, served as the James Welch Distinguished Visiting Professor at University of Montana-Missoula. She lives with her family in Minnesota.

MARITZA N. ESTRADA was born in Toppenish, Washington, to Mexican parents. She earned her MFA in creative writing at Arizona State University and served as the inaugural 2020–21 artistic development and research assistant for the Center for Imagination in the Borderlands at ASU. Estrada is a 2020 CantoMundo Fellow. Her honors and awards include a 2024 CantoMundo Retreat, a

2022 Fortuna artist residency in Mexico City, a Swarthout Award in Poetry, a 2021/2019 Virginia G. Piper Creative Research Fellowship, among others. More of her work can be found in *Narrative*, *The Offing*, *pidgeonholes*, *Blue Mesa Review*, and *Rio Grande Review*.

A. J. EVERSOLE, a citizen of the Cherokee Nation of Oklahoma, grew up in rural Oklahoma, where her imagination flourished through endless games of make-believe. A graduate of Oklahoma State University, she is also a contributor to the anthology *Legendary Frybread Drive-In: Intertribal Stories* and aspires to traditional publication. She lives in Fort Worth, Texas, with her husband and son.

SAMAH SEROUR FADIL is an Afro-Palestinian writer, editor, and translator. Her words can be read in *The Margins*, *Palestine Square*, *Skin Deep*, *Mizna*, *Thyme Travellers: An Anthology of Palestinian Speculative Fiction* and more. Fadil resides in Tiohtià:ke/Montréal.

CHELSEA T. HICKS (she/they) is the author of *A Calm & Normal Heart*, winner of the National Book Foundation's 5 Under 35 Award, and longlisted for the PEN/Robert W. Bingham Prize. A writer, model, and artist, she contemplates rematriation as a form of language and land connection in their work, which has appeared in *Poetry*, *McSweeney's*, *World Literature Today*, *The Paris Review*, and elsewhere. She founded Words of the People to support Indigenous language creative production and reports for *Osage News*. Hicks is Wahzhazhe of the Pawhuska District, Tsizho Washtake Clan, a citizen of the Osage Nation, and a Tulsa Artist Fellowship alumna with degrees from UC Davis and the Institute of American Indian Arts. She is a PhD candidate in interdisciplinary studies at the University of Oklahoma.

DOMINIQUE DAYE HUNTER (she/her) is an Afro-Indigenous (Black, Yeséh/Saponi, Irish and Polish American) storyteller. A poet, author, clothing designer, advocate, and consultant, she is a self-taught artist born and raised in the New York tri-state area. Hunter is the author of *Seeds: Stories of Afro-Indigenous Resilience* and the children's book *Hasí Čhigọyọ*. She holds a BS in nonprofit leadership management (American Indian studies concentration) and is currently pursuing an MFA in creative writing. Hunter resides in Šaunhuntakot (Raleigh-Durham, North Carolina, area).

DARCIE LITTLE BADGER is a Lipan Apache writer with a PhD in oceanography. Her critically acclaimed debut novel, *Elatsoe*, was featured in Time as one of the one hundred best fantasy books of all time. *Elatsoe* also won the Locus Award for Best First Novel and was a finalist for the Nebula Award, the Ignyte Award, and the Lodestar Award. Her second fantasy novel, *A Snake Falls to Earth*, received a Nebula Award, an Ignyte Award, and a Newbery Honor and is on the National Book Awards longlist. *Sheine Lende*, the prequel to *Elatsoe*, is a *USA Today* bestseller. Little Badger is married to a veterinarian named Taran.

PTE SAN WIN LITTLE WHITEMAN is an Oglala Lakota poet who uses poetry for advocacy and healing. Most of their poetry highlights mental health awareness; environmental, racial, and social justice; land/body relationships; and language revitalization. They are an alum of the Brave New Voices and have performed at the Kennedy Center, Native Pop, Black Hills Artist Market, and Poetry Out Loud. Their work has been recognized by *Teen Vogue*, *Indian Country Today*, and *Tribal College Journal of American Indian Higher Education*. Little Whiteman is a youth mentor for NDN Girls Book Club. In their free time, they facilitate workshops, poetry slams, and open mics. They hope to inspire others to read, write, and perform poetry as an act of oral and aural tradition that keeps culture alive and thriving.

CONLEY LYONS is an Indigenous writer of Comanche, German, and Irish descent. She earned a BA in English literature and creative writing from Elon University and an MFA in fiction from the Institute of American Indian Arts. She is currently working on her first novel. Her writing can be found in *Never Whistle at Night*, *Bitch Planet: Triple Feature*, and *them*. Raised in North Carolina's Blue Ridge Mountains, she currently lives in Charlotte, North Carolina.

AMBER MCCRARY is of the Kin Łichíí'nii Clan, born for the Naakaii Dine'é Clan. Her maternal grandfather is of the Áshįįhí Clan, and her paternal grandfather the Ta'neeszahnii Clan. McCrary was born in Tuba City, Arizona, and raised in Flagstaff, Arizona. She is a poet, zinester, tea lover, and dog and cat mom. Her first full collection of poetry, *Blue Corn Tongue: Poems in the Mouth of the Desert*, is out now from the University of Arizona Press. She currently resides on Akimel O'odham lands.

TRISHA MOQUINO is from the Native Nations of Cochiti, Kewa & Ohkay Owingeh. She is a teacher, author, and scholar who co-founded the Keres Children's Learning Center in Cochiti Pueblo, New Mexico, where she serves as a Keres Speaking Montessori Guide for elementary children. In addition to her role at KCLC, Moquino cocreated the Indigenous Montessori Institute and is currently working on several writing projects. Moquino's debut picture book is set to be published by Candlewick Press in 2028. Represented by Lara Perkins at the Andrea Brown Literary Agency, Moquino weaves her passion for education into her writing, bridging the classroom and the page to celebrate and center Native Nations, their lifeways, languages, and Indigenous knowledge systems.

SHAINA A. NEZ is 'Áshįįhi, born for Táchii'nii. Her maternal grandfather's clan is Ta'neeszahnii, and Kin łichii'nii is her paternal grandfather's clan. She is from Lukachukai, Arizona, and currently lives in Mentmore, New Mexico. Nez received her MFA in creative writing from the Institute of American Indian Arts with a focus in creative nonfiction. She has one daughter named Hailee April.

ANDREA L. ROGERS is a citizen of the Cherokee Nation, a mom, a writer, and a teacher. She grew up in Tulsa, Oklahoma, as the oldest of three children. She is the author of *Mary and the Trail of Tears*, *Man Made Monsters*, *When We Gather*, *The Art Thieves*, and *Chooch Helped*. She is a PhD student at the University of Arkansas in Fayetteville and lives near Artists Point. When she's not reading or writing, she may be feeding birds.

HA'ÅNI LUCIA FALO SAN NICOLAS is a CHamoru and Samoan daughter, poet-scholar, activist, and educator from the island of Guåhan. She was among the first fellows cohort of Indigenous Nations Poets in 2022. San Nicolas is also a doctoral candidate in Indigenous politics at the University of Hawai'i at Mānoa and was awarded an inaugural 2023 Mellon/ACLS Dissertation Fellowship to support her research. As a 2023 *Hawai'i Review* artist in residence, she curated and published a poetry collection that features the writing of Indigenous women throughout the Pacific

JAYE SIMPSON (she/they) is an Oji-Cree Saulteaux Indigiqueer from the Sapotaweyak Cree Nation. simpson is a writer, advocate, and activist sharing their knowledge and lived experiences in hopes of creating utopia. Their first poetry collection, *it was never going to be okay* and won the 2021 Indigenous Voices Award for Published Poetry in English..

ARIELLE TWIST is a writer and sex educator from George Gordon First Nation, Saskatchewan, now based in Halifax, Nova Scotia. She is a Nehiyaw, Two-Spirit, trans femme supernova writing to reclaim and harness ancestral magic and memories. Within her short career pursuing writing, she has attended a residency at the Banff Centre for the Arts and Creativity and has work published with *them*, CBC Arts, *Canadian Art*, *The Fiddlehead*, and *PRISM international*. She is the 2020 winner of the Dayne Ogilvie Prize for LGBTQ Emerging Writers from the Writers' Trust of Canada. *Disintegrate/Dissociate*, her first book, won the Indigenous Voices Award for poetry.

AMELIA VIGIL (she/her/they/them) is an Urban-Indigenous/Xicano, Two-Spirit poet, outdoor educator, and identical twin. Their indigenous heritage is Picuris Pueblo from her father and Purepecha from her mother. They have been involved with Bay Area American Indian Two-Spirit (BAAITS) since 2013 and joined the board of directors in 2015. Her advocacy and support of Indigenous self-determination are a constant in their life. Recently appointed the Liberated Paths: Youth Access to Nature (YAN) grant and program manager at Justice Outside, Vigil has earned an MFA in poetry from the Institute for American Indian Arts and degrees from Feather River Community College and Mills College.

CHEYENNE DAKOTA WILLIAMS is a Diné/Naahiłii poet from Virginia. She is Bit'ahnii, born for Naahiłii. Her maternal grandfather's clan is Tódich'ii'nii, and her paternal grandfather's clan Naahiłii. She is currently a student at Fort Lewis College, where she serves as the coeditor in chief for *IMAGES Magazine*. Her poems have been featured in *Yellow Medicine Review*, *Saw Palm*, and *Poetry*. She is an AWP Tribal Colleges & Universities Fellow and a Tin House scholar. Williams spends her time between Virginia and Arizona on the Navajo Nation.

About the Cover Artist

Lynne Hardy is from Arizona and currently resides in Utah. She earned a Bachelor of Arts degree with a minor in Entrepreneurship. Her mediums are digital drawing and painting, created in Adobe Fresco. She describes her work as colorful, modern depictions of her Navajo people and culture. She gains inspiration from her ancestors and wishes to preserve their stories. Authenticity, Native representation, and inclusion are at the heart of her work, as she hopes to share her culture and stop harmful Native stereotypes. In 2020, she launched her small online business named "Ajoobaasani" which sells Navajo products that she creates herself (stickers, prints, and apparel). The launch of "Ajoobaasani" led to opportunities to work with Native-led organizations and companies that needed Native art, allowing her to become a full-time illustrator. Lynne has collaborated with companies such as Google, Yahoo, Adobe, and Visa. A full-time illustrator, Lynne is a contractor for a Navajo language organization. Her other projects include branding for Native small businesses and creating illustrations for marketing purposes. She hopes to continue growing her art career and business, working with clients who value Native culture.

About Torrey House Press

Torrey House Press exists at the intersection of the literary arts and environmental advocacy. THP publishes books that elevate diverse perspectives, explore relationships with place, and deepen our connections to the natural world and to each other. THP inspires ideas, conversation, and action on issues that link the American West to the past, present, and future of the ever-changing Earth.

We believe that lively, contemporary literature is at the cutting edge of social change. We seek to inform, expand, and reshape the dialogue on environmental justice and stewardship for the natural world by elevating literary excellence from diverse voices.

Visit www.torreyhouse.org for reading group discussion guides, author interviews, and more.

As a 501(c)(3) nonprofit publisher, our work is made possible by generous donations from readers like you.

Join the Torrey House Press community and donate today at www.torreyhouse.org/give.

Special Thanks

Beyond the Glittering World **is made possibly by the generous support of Diane Stewart and the Stewart Family Foundation.**

Torrey House Press is supported by Back of Beyond Books, Bright Side Bookshop, The King's English Bookshop, Maria's Bookshop, the Ballantine Family Fund, the Jeffrey S. & Helen H. Cardon Foundation, the Lawrence T. Dee & Janet T. Dee Foundation, the McMullan/O'Connor Family Fund, the Palladium Foundation, the Stewart Family Foundation, the Barker Foundation, Karin Anderson, Kif Augustine & Stirling Adams, Diana Allison, Richard Baker, Karey Barker, Patti Baynham & Owen Baynham, Matt Bean, Klaus Bielefeldt, Joe Breddan, Karen Buchi & Kenneth Buchi, Betty Clark & Gary Clark, Rose Chilcoat & Mark Franklin, Linc Cornell & Lois Cornell, Teow Lim Goh, Susan Cushman & Charlie Quimby, Lynn de Freitas & Patrick de Freitas, Pert Eilers, Ed Erwin, Laurie Hilyer, Phyllis Hockett, John Hueston, Kirtly Parker Jones, Emily Klass, Rick Klass, Jen Lawton & John Thomas, Matthew Lindon, Susan Markley, Leigh Meigs & Stephen Meigs, Mark Meloy, Kathleen Metcalf, Donaree Neville & Douglas Neville, Laura Paskus, Katie Pearce, Marion S. Robinson, Linnea Spears-Lebrun, Jennifer Speers, Molly Swonger, Shelby Tisdale, Rachel White, the National Endowment for the Humanities, the National Endowment for the Arts, the Utah Division of Arts & Museums, Utah Humanities, the Salt Lake City Arts Council, and Salt Lake County Zoo, Arts & Parks. Our thanks to individual donors, members, and the Torrey House Press board of directors for their valued support.